Centaur of the North

Stories
by
Wendell Mayo

Arte Público Press
Houston, Texas
1996

This volume is made possible through grants from the National Endowment for the Arts (a federal agency), Andrew W. Mellon Foundation, and the Lila Wallace Reader's-Digest Fund.

Recovering the past, creating the future

Arte Público Press
University of Houston
Houston, Texas 77204-2090

Cover design by Gladys Ramirez
Cover art "Accompanied by Sunflowers and Patience"
by Nivia Gonzalez

Mayo, Wendell.
    Centaur of the North / by Wendell Mayo.
        p.   cm.
    Contents: The stone kitchen — Conquistador — El centauro del Norte — The banker's son — La villa, la villa miseria — Soledad — New moon — El ojo — Corpus.
    ISBN 1-55885-165-8 (paper : alk. paper)
    1. Mexican American families—Southwestern States—Fiction. 2. Southwestern States—Social life and customs—Fiction. I. Title.
PS3563.A9644C46   1996
813'.54—dc20   96-16943
                                                CIP

The paper used in this publication meets the requirements of the American National Standard for Permanence of Paper for Printed Library Materials Z39.48-1984. ∞

Acknowledgments

"Soledad" previously appeared in *Prairie Schooner*, Fall 1994; "El Centauro del Norte" in *High Plains Literary Review*, Spring 1995, and reprinted in *Westview*; "The Stone Kitchen" in *New Letters*, Winter 1994 (as first-runner up in the National New Letters Literary Awards); "The Banker's Son" in *Western Humanities Review*, Summer 1995; "Conquistador" in *Western Humanities Review*, Fall 1993, and reprinted in *Louisiana English Journal*; "La Villa, La Villa Miseria" in *Chattahoochee Review*, Winter 1992; "New Moon" in *Dickinson Review*, Spring 1989; "Corpus" in *American Writing*, Winter 1992; and "El Ojo" in *New Delta Review*, Fall 1995 (as winner of the Eyster Prize).

In appreciation of their support, the author would like to thank Yaddo, the Millay Colony for the Arts, and the Indiana Arts Commission.

Contents

For on every continent,
in every country, however small,
there is something extra
that does not belong there.

—Fabio Morábito, "The Last of the Tribe"

Centaur
of the
North

The Stone Kitchen

While she was alive, Silvia and I never shared a language. Not really—and there were other matters between us, I mean "between" not that we had other matters in common, but there seemed to be something intervening, something we pushed away from us, only to find our words broken or hesitant, our little stories barely believable, like little stones of irregular shapes, never fitting together in even the most approximate way.

Some of these little misshapen stones were obvious. Silvia was my mother, a biological fact that separated us twenty years, something not to be avoided, though I'll admit we must have had a good nine months or so together at the outset. I'm sure she remembered; I do not. But there was another matter: her being a woman, only this never seemed to bother me until I became much older, now a man, as men are, whatever that is, and, regrettably, seemed to connect her queer little ways with womanhood, or everything that is not manhood...and I was wrong, do not know why, can only guess, but would rather do my best to stick to the facts...

When I was ten, she and Father had come with me, their only child, from the sweltering South, Corpus Christi, the Gulf, a place of sand and broken white sea shells, of heat and a kind of bluish, fermented slowness of the body, a warmth within warmth that felt like family, different than the feel of family in our final destination, a suburb north of Chicago.

Father, as I remember him here in Chicago, never seemed as intrigued as I did about Silvia's strange ways. He was a tolerant man with other concerns, the kind of tolerance that allowed for everything, but never quite included it. Father and I had no stories between us, nothing in our way; he was a quiet, accepting man, with a modest job like most men, the manager of an IGA supermarket.

But Silvia did not have Father's quiet clarity. For example, she chattered hours in Spanish with her mother, Luisa, who had remained behind in Corpus. Of course, I asked for lessons in Spanish and was promised them, but they never came. And my mother's name itself, *Silvia*, was another instance, the smallest pebble, almost invisible, yet plainly felt, like a small rock that had worked its way into an inaccessible corner of my shoe: *Silvia* was the name I have put back to its original spelling since Mother, all the while I knew her, had dropped the 'i' and replaced it with 'y', thus *Sylvia*. But I have traced her, pursued her through her papers, certificates of birth and marriage. I have put the 'i' back into her name in my own way, knowing it is more Spanish, as if my pathetic little attempt would somehow renew her, her memory, my memory of her as she worked in her kitchen, the most puzzling stone of all, the stone kitchen as I knew it in those days.

When we first moved north to Chicago, Silvia's kitchen had been like other kitchens, with long, clean white Formica counters, cupboards hanging above them, a range, refrigerator, an automatic dishwasher. But as months passed in our new home, Silvia transformed the kitchen into something strange and fantastic. She stuffed the oven with empty coffee tins of beans and flour. She strung garlic and jalapeños around the window casings. She brought in pots of basil and parsley plants, set them on the floor or hung them on hooks from the ceiling, so low to the floor that I found myself ducking as I came into the kitchen. She stored more tins of beans, kernel corn, lettuce, and potatoes in the dishwasher.

She used the refrigerator, an Admiral, for some things, meats, but more often than not, summer nights, she'd shut down the central air conditioning and I'd see her standing in the open door of the Admiral, its feeble white light, wiping an ice cube over her face and rocking the door back and forth on its hinges, fanning herself.

Silvia received many stone pots—one large pot she called her *olla*—all in the mail from Corpus. She gathered grinding bowls and crudely cut wooden spoons which she strew over the stove and counters. And Silvia saved bacon and sausage grease—all of it—which she poured into other empty coffee cans and reused. She would scrape the grease out with two fingers and smear the bottoms of her great iron skillets; when she put the gas flame under the skillets, the grease would smoke and smell horribly. In these skillets she'd make tortillas, heart, tongue, *tripas*, *huevos*—and other combinations—heart and pintos, tongue and pintos, *tripas* and pintos, pintos and pintos...

A warm autumn day, the postman came to our door. He was panting. His knees were red and bent slightly, and between them in both hands he carried a large flat object shaped like an egg, wrapped in brown paper. I took the heavy package from him and rolled it along its oblong edges to get it into the living room. The postmark was *Corpus Christi, Texas*, the package from Luisa, and it had cost a small fortune to mail. Silvia came up to me, pointed at her kitchen, and said, "No... put it in there." So I did; we both lifted the package and set it on the counter; she unwrapped the package very slowly and deliberately, as if she knew what it was—a large flat brown chopping stone, rough and pebbled on one side and smooth on the other. She wiped both sides with a damp cloth, set it carefully on the counter, and left the kitchen.

So for me Silvia's kitchen became the stone kitchen, a strange mélange of modern baked-white enamel peeping around rocks and foliage, her *olla*, her great brown chopping stone, and what I considered other primitive elements, old smoky grease, her odd, alien ways.

A cold morning, a cold I could tell was getting at Silvia in her kitchen, she wore her handmade yarn slippers, Father's jeans, two shirts, a windbreaker, and stocking cap. I sat at the table, watching her, and it seemed to me it wasn't all that cold; it was a bit chilly in the corners of the house where the wind swept through the tiniest cracks and caused little icy eddies against the arm—but Silvia communicated another kind of coldness, even if only through her apparel. Layered with clothes, she greased her great hot skillet, and strings of smoke rose from it into the electric exhaust hood over the range, a gadget she never used because, "This doesn't work so well." So she opened the window over the sink near the range, and stood fanning the strings of smoke out. She flapped her arms and huffed. After a time I heard a kind of groan come through her tight lips, a small sound forbearing the exertion and the chill that had suddenly transformed her kitchen into a hazy icebox.

I leaned back a little in my chair and glanced up the stairs just outside the kitchen that led to the bedrooms on the second floor of our house, fearing that Father would be right down to scold us both for wasting heat, but I heard him in the shower, the water running in the pipes, and all I could think was that Silvia had the oddest ways of going about things, so I continued to watch her with intense curiosity.

She huffed again, blowing a few strands of black hair away from her round brownish face; then she lowered the open window to just a crack, broke three eggs, scrambled them in a bowl, and poured them into a skillet. She dumped half a bag of Fritos into the eggs, stirred, peppered them, and dished them into a bowl with a crude wooden spoon.

"What do you call that?" I asked her.

"I don't call it nothing," she said, setting the bowl containing the concoction on the table in front of me. "I call it breakfast—*eat*."

I glanced again upstairs, wondering if I could hold out long enough to get a second opinion from Father, but Silvia stared at me a short while, began to tap her toe on the linoleum, then nervously busied herself with things in the kitchen. She fussed with a basket of chili peppers she'd gotten the day before, threading them together with string, then looping them through the handle of the refrigerator door. Then she dusted her tomatoes with a cotton cloth, dozens of them lining the window sills and counters. When she turned to look at me again and tap her toe, I had no choice. I'd stalled long enough, so I stabbed into the concoction and tasted it.

I have heard that the mind can partially block and restructure taste, so mine did. I don't know now if it had been the wise thing to do; I must have missed some things in my early life, Silvia's cooking, some unusual and exotic tastes; but I could, when it seemed Silvia was experimenting with meals or using up "old stuff," as she called it, separate the tastes into their individual parts, an intellectual trick, to individuate everything for digestion and block the full effect of something rather unknown. Even as a child I'd trained myself to do this, though I wonder now if it had been all so wise, wonder if knowing about all things in a kind of fearful individuation excludes other matters.

Before Silvia's disappointed, half-busied gaze could urge me to take another bite of the concoction, Father came down the stairs and into the kitchen, said not a word, rubbed the tips of his elbows with his hands, put his nose slightly up in the air, swallowed a little coffee, and started out the side door to go to work. But Silvia, who had been watching him the whole time, said to his back:

"Well!... Well!... I know this kitchen is full of smoke! I know it's cold! But how can you expect me to cook when I can't open this window?"

Father gave her his most tolerant smile, reached into the bowl with the concoction in it, took a bit of it in his fingers and ate it. Then he kissed her sweetly and left. I took a couple bites of my egg and soggy corn chips just to fill the silence and avoid Silvia's stare, which turned first to the doorway Father had just gone through, then to me. I got up and walked slowly to the hood over the range and, quickly, before she was on to me, sprung up on my toes and pressed the button to run the fan.

The fan hummed. Her eyes moved from the fan, to me, and back to the fan. She was holding her breath, so I said, "Why don't you use the fan like Father showed you?"

In my ten years, it was the bravest thing I'd ever said, so I stood there with Silvia in a kind of vacuum, unsure of my future, and trembled a little, but Silvia suddenly exhaled, sighed, swept a lock of her dark hair from her face, and tucked it under her stocking cap.

"Listen," she said, looking tired, "I don't want you to talk about me—now, or when I'm dead. The dead do not like gossip."

"Are you going to die?"

"No," she said. "I mean, yes, so remember what I told you."

Silvia came over, rose high on her toes, for she was a tiny woman, and pushed the off switch on the fan. The kitchen was suddenly calm, silent.

"Promise?" she asked.

So I promised.

So Silvia and I had this kind of pact, but it changed over the years, as I grew older and started to make older friends, girlfriends, boyfriends, friends who would ask me about my parents. Father was easy: "He manages a supermarket." But with Silvia, I drew a blank, and even then I did not want my friends to reply in ways that seemed embarrassing, such as, "Oh, she's a housewife?" And I could not bring myself to say, "My mom? She's nice—pretty." Nothing I could conjure up quite described her, even to myself, so what was I to tell others? So, then, in my teens, I asked Silvia,

"I know I'm not supposed to talk about you, but people ask. What should I tell them?"

She was chopping an incongruous mixture of heart, tongue, onion, and corn on her big flat stone; she stopped a moment, rapping the butt of the chopping knife on the counter and thinking.

"All right, here's what we'll say. Tell them this story: When I was a little girl in Guatemala, I remember a young woman coming to our town from the Peace Corps. She was pretty, with long, straight blonde hair that went down to her waist." Silvia reached around to her back and pointed at her waist with the tip of the chopping knife. "Here, you see—? Well, the woman from the Peace Corps came to help us with our economy. That is how the woman said it, *economy*. So many of us, my parents included, thought this was a good idea, and we showed her all the things we could grow or make to help with the economy. We showed her some of the beautiful little dolls we made with painted stone faces, straw, and bits of cloth and threads with many colors in them. But the woman from the Peace Corps said, reaching for a clay pot my mother had made, 'Let's make these. You can paint the stone faces of the dolls on them if you want to.'

"So, for a while we made these clay pots, and put only the faces of the dolls on them, but gradually no one in my town made the pots anymore, so our economy never improved. And the woman asked my father one day, 'Why won't you make the pots?' And my mother said before my father could speak, 'Because we like to make the dolls; they are pretty; they are not like pots; they are like little people.' And when the woman said, 'But we can't sell these dolls!' my mother laughed and asked her if she wanted some supper with us."

Silvia went back to chopping heart and tongue, and I went away feeling I had finally learned a little about Silvia, enough for the time being, though when I tried her little story out on even my closest friends, they said they didn't get it. Was it some kind of joke? So, in a curious way, Silvia's story seemed to wash out what I assumed were the new facts I'd come to possess about her—her place of birth, her family, her odd ways. And this was the first episode in a puzzling game we played over the next few years, a game that began when I'd say something like this to Silvia:

"I told So And So your story about the dolls, but So And So didn't get it—what else can I tell So And So?"

I partly asked her this because I half-thought she enjoyed hearing me ask, and my asking came at a time when she'd become, in those later days, what I could only assume was homesick for Corpus Christi. She was then on the telephone a couple times every week with Luisa in Corpus, which seemed to make things tense in the house when the phone bills came, though Father, ever the silent ghost of tolerance, said nothing. He also said nothing about Silvia's partially transforming a corner of the kitchen by the pantry into a mess of magazines sprawled over the buffet and onto the linoleum. Some magazines made sense to me, the pictures in them, such as *National Geographic*, but others did not, such as *Gente*, *Tu Internacional*, *Mundo 21*, and *Padres y Hijos*. But they too seemed significant, since I became convinced that somehow homesickness and loneliness were related to indecipherable magazines...

I also hoped that Silvia's telling me one more story of her childhood might give *her* a kind of relief; so I found her again working in her kitchen and asked her to tell me another. She replied, "All right, forget about the dolls and Guatemala." She paused a moment and ran her tongue over her lower lip, as if in deep thought. She wiped corn-flour dough off her hands, and, as she appeared to be thinking, I watched her make the dough into tiny yellow balls and set them in a row on her brown chopping stone. "Tell them... tell them that when I was a little girl in Pozzuoli, Italy, my family lived in a small stone house near the sea. One day there was a great blast in the volcano, Vesuvio, above. Fire came down out of the sky like rain. We began to choke on the dust, and we ran for our lives.... Finally, we were safe and stayed with relatives in Napoli nearby. Weeks later we went back to our house by the sea in Pozzuoli, but the roof was burned off and the windows broken out and everything inside was ashes. Only the stone walls remained. My father didn't say anything. My mother cried, so I cried, and even my older brother, Augusto, he cried. So we went back to Napoli, away from Pozzuoli, and lived there.

"When I grew to be a young woman, in my teens like you, I got a job. My brother, Augusto, also had a job and moved out of the house into his own apartment. One day, my father and mother and I went back to the stone house with no windows or roof in Pozzuoli. Father had never sold it. We had made a basket of food. There, we ate our lunches in silence, wine, bread, cheese, some pasta, and when we'd finished, what do you know? Augusto was there standing in the hole where the door had been burned away, and when we saw him, we cried; he cried; and we all talked and had more wine and made a pledge we would always meet Tuesdays for lunch at the stone house with no roof or windows in Pozzuoli by the sea—and we did—even in the rain."

Silvia tossed some hard corn into her stone bowl and began to grind it; she had her back to me, slightly hunched, an attitude that told me I should not say anything—I should not, from the position of her back, look to see her expression as she mashed the corn.

I couldn't even begin to think about telling Silvia's new story to my friends, especially friends I had known a long while and who would hear both her stories. Her incongruous stories silenced me. The stack of magazines in the corner of her kitchen continued to puzzle me, and began to include newspapers. It grew into a great, gray and glossy pile, and now included *Paris Match*, *¡Hola!*, and *Hombre Internacional*. Like her stories and reading materials, I began to regard her with suspicion. Nights, I watched her closely as she sat in front of the television, often watching a ballet, opera, or travelogue on PBS. And after a time, though I sensed that the story of Guatemala and of Pozzuoli were both lies, the lies seemed to bring us closer. Unlike most self-respecting teen-agers, I stayed near my mother out of sheer curiosity, hoping that just once she'd break out of her hard kernel of silence and absurdity and lay herself bare to me like slivers of heart and tongue on her chopping stone. I needed a story I could believe.

But none came, and in desperation bordering on resentment, which I'd never felt before for Silvia, didn't want to believe I could, I went to Father with her two stories, and he replied in his most tolerant tone, "Don't worry. That's just your mama telling stories. She's from Corpus, born and raised there..."

At first I was satisfied with Father's explanation, but I soon realized I wanted a story from *her*, and in my own resentful way, I wanted a true story—and it had to come from *her*. Maybe I wanted this because of what she'd said about dying and gossip—perhaps she'd be gone soon, then what would I have to show for all my trouble over the years? But I also felt I was persisting in my inquiry for her sake. I wanted to be her sympathetic, understanding listener, but how could I when she told such outrageous stories? I wanted to break through the code of her indecipherable past and my puzzling curiosity, but how could I when she lied and lied so?

I thought briefly about confronting her with the obvious incongruities in her two stories, and with the added confidence of Father's disclosure, confrontation made sense. I would simply force her to tell me the truth. But then I started thinking about Silvia *herself*. She'd just as soon chop and put her back at me as breathe. Her chopping heart and tongue, her grinding corn, her stories upon stories, all I'd come to know about her, were a kind of language themselves, one of stories, I believed lies, and silence—but why? So my only recourse was simple, all that was left to me, considering Silvia as Silvia, and when I'd at last found her in her stone kitchen rolling wheat dough out on her great flat stone, I said, innocently, "Mama, tell me another story about when you were a girl." I figured that the more stories I could get out of her, no matter how imaginative, the more material I'd have to sort through. At least I'd then have something in which I could look for common themes, threads, motifs—anything to make it all make sense. But I had to be sure she'd give me a good story, so I added, "Make it about *you*, Mama, just about *you*."

Then I wondered if what I had just said might have tipped her to my intent and silence her all together, but Silvia set her rolling pin aside and leaned against her great stone. She shook a bit of white flour off her fingers and said, "There was an old doctor in Vermont—"

"Vermont?"

"Yes, Vermont...don't interrupt me...do you want to hear this?"

"Yes."

"All right," she paused, I supposed to collect her thoughts. "This old doctor in Vermont, near North Bennington, was a doctor a long time ago, not like doctors now. You could bring anything to him for doctoring—birds, animals, people—even a fish from one of the mountain streams. He lived alone in a small wooden shack on a small rocky hill overlooking the village. He never had a sweetheart, or a wife, or children, so he was very lonely, but he was used to it because he'd been like that his whole life.

"All right, this old doctor...when someone or something was sick in the village, he would hitch his horse to his wagon and go to help them. When he finished his doctoring, when he was by himself on his way up the small hill to his shack, he would stop many times and search the sides of the road for rocks. He had a wire hoop with him about this size," Silvia put her hands together and made a circle about the size of a cantaloupe, "and he would take each rock and see if it would just fit through the hoop. If the rock fit, he put it in his wagon. Some people from the village saw the old man gathering the rocks and eventually they would ask him, 'What are you doing with these rocks?' but he wouldn't tell them; he would just make some excuse, like, 'I collect them,' or 'I need them for a counterweight in the well.'

"After the old doctor of birds and fish and people and animals died in his shack on the hill, the people of the village soon discovered that he had built a beautiful house hidden in a clearing behind the wooden shack. The house was made of all the stones he had collected over many years. The people were amazed by this, but sad because they believed he had never lived in the house it took him so long to build before he died..."

Silvia put her back to me again, but this time not in an attitude of silence, of pushing me away. In the light coming through the window over her sink, I saw her shoulder blades go together and tremble, there, framed in the window with her garlands of chiles and baskets of onions. Then, I suddenly felt the faintest stirrings of what she might have been saying...but I was pernicious as a youth and I blurted out, "But it's not about you..."

Her shoulder blades suddenly relaxed and I heard her sigh.

"It is—it is about me—it's all about me!" she said.

As far as I'll ever know, Silvia never settled for one story of her childhood, and as time went on she told me others as we grew older, as we wondered, paused, and learned to make a little laughter together about them. But Silvia never relented. She persisted in her fictions, and I never took any of her stories and made them my own, never bound them together into

a bundle, never believed I could make a bright metal nugget of
truth from what I believed were clods of clay.

Now the house in the suburb north of Chicago is mine.
Silvia went first from cancer ten years ago, Father only two
from heart failure. Since he had lived in the house alone after
Silvia's passing away, her stone kitchen is gone, her garlands,
her *olla*, her skillet grease and clouds of smoke, the potted
parsley and basil. At the last, her heap of magazines and
newspapers included *El País* and *El Mundo* and *Su Futuro*.
But I have let the subscriptions expire, and only her big brown
chopping stone remains, rough on one side, smooth on another. It feels good in my hands, either side, the rough, pebbly
one something akin to her stories, her crazy ways, the smooth
one more about her chopping I hear time to time over the
years, a kind of chopping of everything she'd prepared for me,
a language of heart and tongue, incongruous meats and
sounds...but all in all, through it all, chopping and stone.

Only one story of hers ever seemed to be of consequence
for me, my life, in even the vaguest way, one of Silvia as a little girl, living near Kunming in China, a Sani village among
limestone formations in fantastic shapes, sprawling in
labyrinthine patterns of narrow paths through crevices in the
rocks. Silvia called it the Stone Forest, where great islands of
rocks, like apparitions, rose out of the Sani rice fields, the neat
rows of green seedlings. The legend, she said, was that one of
China's eight immortals shattered a mountain to make the
labyrinth for lovers to wander inside.... And Silvia added how
as a little girl she loved to sit hours by one rock precariously
perched upon another, called Hanging by a Hair, and I
laughed when she told me this, felt myself lost in the Stone
Forest with her, believed with the precision of a dream that
two rocks could be so delicately balanced upon one another.
For a moment I again felt the glimmer of belief in my
heart...her place in the world, my place...somewhere behind
my eyes where the image lingered...but it soon faded
there...a ghost...

Since Silvia passed away, I have broken my promise to
her. I tell people about her, her ways, and what it is I think I
cannot know. To some I say I am her child, her only child,
bewildered child with heart and tongue of stone. To others I
simply give a good lie, one among many I have of my mother.
Perhaps the dead do not like gossip, but is this the worst kind
of gossip? To want these stones to give up their secrets? So,
nights, alone, in what is now my house, I beg what I remember of the stones and garlands of Silvia's kitchen to talk a little to one another so that I may listen in. I tip her big
chopping stone on its end and press my palms to both surfaces
at once, knowing that only in dreams can such a praying as
this make a single sensation in the tender parts of my hands,
my tongue, my heart, no matter how remote or incomplete.

Conquistador

The heroes of the world have been feared and admired.

—Martin Decoud, *Nostromo*

Summer nights, ghost crabs come into Corpus Christi, clamber up the rocks and swagger across the sands from the east bay, north to the tiny islands of the archipelago, Mustang Island, and still further south to San Padre Island, where they come onto the laps of shallow coves in droves, and in the moonlight, a soft, strange violet light, their bodies reach the near point of translucence. Their presence here is a silent contradiction: the mind conceives of the hard armor carapaces over their backs and broad, jutting chests, yet their images in the night light are soft and strange, like spirits wandering onto shore to meet other spirits, to whisper among themselves of their other lives in tidal pools, or to speak of their cousins, the blue crabs, who live many months in the deeper, darker parts of the Gulf, in another watery terrain, perhaps the sunken, shifting hull of a Spanish galleon, or in the skull of a drowned sea captain, or among the itinerant bones of my grandfather's ancestor, Francisco Durante, that ancient captain of the Spanish Main whose name my grandfather reportedly took from him, as my grandmother Eva tells it.

I have also seen droves of fiddlers near the salt marshes as they tack across the compacted sandy mud among blades of sea grass, each carrying its absurdly proportioned chela high like a diminutive soldier wielding a lance; but I have always walked alone with the ghosts and fiddlers, always without

Eva or Francisco, and without my parents who were lost to me in consecutive years: my father in 1962 when his rig loaded with pipe string headed for the Anadarko Gas Fields went off the road outside Tivoli; my mother in 1963 to cancer. So I belonged to Eva on my father's side when I was nine years of age, and from that time on I became a conquistador, a product of old ways, so Eva told me: her dead husband, she explained, was the descendant of Francisco Durante...*el conquistador*.... *Someday*, she said, *you will be anything you want.*

We lived on Old Brownsville Road in a small white house like many of the houses dotting the outlying areas of Corpus, in and around the groves of pecan trees and fields of cotton. The house was a square single story, with a tar-paper roof, bubbled and peeling siding, and a dark, forbidding crawl space under the back porch. The kitchen was located directly to the right of the back door at the porch. A single window permitted light to fall in a square over the sink, a low black gas range, a small table, and plank shelf fixed halfway up the opposite wall, upon which the entire assortment of Eva's cookery rested: several wooden spoons, a deep cast iron skillet, a flat stone platter, a wooden rolling pin, and a stone pot Eva called her *olla* and in which she cooked *olla podrida*. Several knives my grandfather had peened, tempered, and sharpened also lay scattered between the pots and pans. In another corner of the tiny kitchen Eva kept empty coffee tins for flour, beans, rice, corn—and one for her old chicken bones she used for crabbing at the breakwater in Corpus Christi Bay.

Eva and I took our meals at a small square table in the center of the kitchen, not in the larger dining room where Francisco had eaten his meals. Eva explained to me that this was tradition, and that tradition was important to a conquistador. But I believed that Eva set our table in the kitchen out of habit, or because she was somehow more comfortable there.

One day, soon after I came to live with Eva, she said, "Someday you will head a great table of your own.... You will have a loving wife and many *niños y niñas*."

From that day on, knowing that Francisco and she had dined in two rooms in the same house, I began to feel separate from Eva. But even with my sense of separateness, I followed Eva everywhere in my first days with her. We were each with our own recent losses—she, her Francisco, me with my father and mother. I trailed her into the back yard, and to the small coop she kept at the side of Francisco's tool shed. I watched her reach in and pull a chicken out by its legs. She carried the struggling bird to the back porch as if she were walking onto a stage. She took the chicken by the neck, swung it over her head in a wide circle—and snapped her wrist and its neck at the same time. I was amazed that her small, brown, wrinkled hands could so suddenly take the life of anything. Yet my astonishment soon vanished in the shadow of Francisco Durante. Evenings, she would kneel by Francisco's chest, take out his First World War clothes, helmet, medals, and rusty bayonet, and spread them all on the bed:

"He was a brave man, your grandfather Francisco."

Of course, I mulled over this business of being a conquistador, as children ponder things of such importance. Eva's assertion that I was a conquistador was incongruous with my surroundings. How could such an important man as Francisco Durante have left his wife in such modest circumstances? A tiny tar-papered house on a broken asphalt strip one dared to call "road," just "Old Brownsville?" Still, I was interested in her remarks about conquistadors and bravery, so I sat and thought about it while feeding her chickens, and later drawing stick figures in the dust across Old Brownsville. One afternoon I announced my conclusions to Eva as she stood in the kitchen stirring pintos in her old stone pot: if I was indeed a conquistador, then it was my wish to be a great treasure hunter, and to find the sunken galleon my great ancestor had captained.

"Oh," Eva said, "you will find many riches in the Gulf, and you will become a famous treasure hunter."

But though I wanted to believe her, her appearance made me suspicious. Eva was such a tiny woman, with a flat rump, a small waist, short dark hair, and a flat smooth nose. Her skin was olive-green, and her hair coal-black, not like mine. I never bothered her about her ancestors because it was obvious, even to so young a boy in Corpus Christi, that she was Mexican... more precisely Mexican Indian. It was this that kept me from believing her about my more important ancestors, those of Francisco Durante, but she pulled the wooden spoon out of her *olla* and set it aside.

"Look," she said, and she reached for something on the window ledge over her sink. She handed me a small coin, deeply worn and tarnished gray. "A diver found this many years ago," she said. "The diver said he found it at the wreck of *El Aliento*."

El Aliento was the elder Francisco's fabled galleon, part of, Eva said, a Spanish treasure fleet of twenty ships beset by a hurricane and lost off Padre Island in 1553. I turned the coin over and over in my hand. I made out the letters *CINCO PESOS* on one side of the coin, and the vague image of a dragon-like animal on the other side.

"Is it gold?" I asked her.

"*Sí, sí,*" she laughed, "*el oro.*"

I did not know at the time if she kidded me or not, but it didn't matter. Eva bought a pair of diving goggles, and we took her dead Francisco's old pale-green Ford Falcon to the breakwater, with two fishing poles and a bucket of old chicken bones Eva saved from several meals.

I am never sure if it was more my imagination, but Corpus Christi Bay that day—my christening as a great treasure hunter—was blue and deep as the sky. The bay, as I knew it,

had many moods—gray, green, or brown-green in the winter
when the jellyfish came in and left themselves in the low tide
like gelatin buttons over stretches of beach. But this day the
surface of the bay under the glow of the sun in the cloudless
sky was passionately blue. The breakwater ran through the
bay like the white, scaly back of a great serpent, bending
away from the sea wall in a lazy *S* north toward Aransas Pass
and the Gulf. And I believed I possessed unfathomable
strength, like that of a magnificent serpent. I believed I could
put my arms the whole way around one of the large palms
leaning over the beach and climb to the top of it in an instant,
and there see as no man has ever before—as no one would
ever again—all the lands and seas of my domain.

I left Eva a short distance out on the breakwater with her
bucket of bones and fishing poles, and raced around it to the
beach, to a spot just north of the pilings at the pier nearby.

I slipped on my new goggles, put my chest out, and
skipped into the surf until I felt the sea full and deep around
me. I knifed through the swells beyond the breaking flat
sheets of froth, and bore into the next swell and the next.... I
was the great treasure hunter, and I tore open the water with
my skull and stuck my eyes in their goggles to the task of
looking into the sea, yet I saw only bits of debris and the most
murky sorts of shapes coming and going in my field of vision.
I came up for air, saw Eva wave to me from the breakwater
beyond the pier, then felt, as I was at the very height of my
disappointment, dozens of impressions on my body—as if
many fingers touched me all over, all at once—and around me
I saw a myriad of tiny splashes, like a thousand pebbles suddenly dashed into the water. I tore for the shore with both
arms sailing around me like the vanes of a windmill, and
raced through the surf back to the beach. There I removed my
goggles and threw them onto the sand.

I sat for a time watching Eva baiting her poles, then I
slowly walked back to her on the breakwater.

"Well," she said, tugging at the line of one pole with her index finger, "have you found Francisco's treasure?"

I sat and took the other pole in my lap.

"Not yet," I said.

"Someday, you will," she said, and pulled up a blue crab with her pole, its claw clamped around the smaller broken half of a wishbone. She dropped the crab into her bucket, cut the line, then smiled and pointed at the spot in the water from which I had just fled. The surface of the water suddenly broke and thousands of tiny rifts appeared then vanished. "So many little fish."

I ignored Eva's enthusiasm for the bounty of the sea, and instead pointed to the crab, which was pressing its hard greenish claws, its legs and paddles, all simultaneously against the sides of the bucket. The crab turned itself round and round.

"He is so stupid," I said to Eva. "All he wants is that stupid wishbone, and he never lets it go—even when you pull him in, all the way out of the sea." When I said this, Eva looked surprised, but she set about tying another chicken bone on her line, and I added, "He deserves to die."

I am never sure if Eva felt this was a horrible thing for me to say. She never mentioned it. We caught six more crabs that afternoon, boiled and ate them that night, and Eva said to me, "Some day you will be very smart—a doctor or a painter. I will be so proud of you."

She put her hand on my shoulder and I ran from her into my room. I am not certain if I fled because I was ashamed of my cowardice in the face of the vicious little fishes, or if, somehow, Eva's premonitions about my future—my being a conquistador—set me forever above her. After all, compared to the boy my father's blood and his father's blood had brought forth, what was she? A tiny Indian woman who caught crabs with old dried chicken bones and stood in the tiny square of light made by the narrow window in her kitchen and boiled pintos and *podrida* in her old stone *olla* all day for my meals.

But I was the grandson of Francisco Durante, who was the descendant and namesake of a daring captain of the Spanish Main—who might have become, had not the fortunes of adventure sunk him in the Gulf, a famous soldier, doctor, or artisan in his time.

Eva did not immediately come to find me in my room. I suspect she sensed the difference between my blood and her blood and stayed away. Still, I reasoned, she was part of me, the small boyish part, and though I was sure I would soon shed this part of myself—of her—it made me think a long while about my mother and father in the only way I could bear their loss: they were in Heaven together, happier than I ever knew them to be, happier than I would ever be here in Corpus, here in this humid, slow old patch of seaside dust and rock. I had to, somehow, strike out from here, even if it meant joining them in their afterlives...yet Eva's words kept coming to me, *someday, someday*, and others, *wait, not yet...*

Later that evening, I stood in Francisco's dining room and watched Eva in her kitchen plucking the chicken for tomorrow's dinner; she was whispering to the chicken in Spanish...*lo siento*...and pulling its feathers with her tiny worn hands with great care and tenderness, which seemed to me a foolish thing to do since the bird was stone-cold dead.

Eva did not mention how rough this whole business of being a conquistador could be. She had plans for me, and now that I began to accept my destiny as a great conqueror, she set her plans in motion—she must have, that is, because her preparations seemed so queer—and her plans seemed to me far above even my expectations of a conquistador, certainly far above those parents had of other boys I knew at school. Naturally, Spanish was not taught at school, so Eva taught me the Spanish of the Royal Academy in Spain, which never failed to get me in trouble with my friends who, rather than thinking me regal or refined, simply did not understand me, or laughed at my clumsy use of *vosotros* instead of *ustedes*. Eva bought a paint set, an easel, and glittering paints of lapis lazuli, gold and silver, and rich blacks and purples. I painted Spanish galleons, though I had never seen one: bark-like crafts with crooked, angular sails and ridiculous stick men on their decks. Later, she gave me a book with illustrations and I copied the ships as best I could. Still, from my early failures to my poor duplications of ships of the Spanish Armada, she would stand by the easel, cross her arms over her chest, and sigh, "Oh, these are lovely—you see, you see!"

I am never sure what she saw or expected me to see, but all of my training seemed innocuous enough, with the possible exception of my use of the King's Spanish with the boys at school, which I remedied by simply speaking differently with them.

But other matters of my training were more painful. I was confirmed and made First Communion late since my father and mother had never gotten to it, but Eva could not see the least bit embarrassment in it. I stood a head higher than all the other children at First Communion Mass, and the whole matter of kneeling was foreign to me; I did so shakily, and only after all the other children kneeled obediently. Perhaps if I had been younger I would not have felt such resistance.... I was sure the priest paused and smiled before he laid the wafer on my tongue. I had forgotten to hold my hands at my sides, and I *reached* for it...

Eva was deeply moved: "You are with God now. He is with you now, forever."

I was too young to feel the deep mysteries of faith and, unlike the other children of six and seven, too old to believe the whole matter just plain fun. But it was good to know God was with me, especially that next week at school when I punched out George Ramírez for calling me an orphan. Eva came to school and sat by my side in the principal's office. She looked sadly at the principal, Mr. Lynch, with her big brown eyes.

"He's a good boy.... He just lost his father and his mother.... He's a good boy."

Whatever Eva did, whatever special quality of voice or manner she possessed, she got me out of many scrapes at school. The other children tortured me for not having parents; but I believed older people were easy, and with time I could slug any kid for saying anything; I would suffer only a royal scolding from Mr. Lynch, then Eva would come to rescue me. God was with me, and I suppose with His help I won a kind of victory: eventually none of the children would say anything to me—only the most obligatory and polite salutations.

A year passed, and I had no more a notion of what it was to be the son of a son of a son...of a son of a conquistador than the Man in the Moon. I was old enough then to study the great explorers: Balboa, Cortez, Pizarro, Ponce de León, as well as Alonso Alvarez de Piñeda, who reportedly first sighted and named the city on the day of Corpus Christi in 1519. Yet even this historical fact baffled me. Had Piñeda the honor of first sight? No one can say he *saw* Corpus Christi, and what if he had been looking at something else all together? Later that year in school we learned that the French explorer René Robert Cavelier, sieur de La Salle, perhaps sailed by Corpus Christi in 1685—had *he* been keeping his eyes peeled? Or had Alonso de León seen the bay on two trips while chasing after the Frenchman La Salle?—or was it the English?—Ingram, Bourne, and Twide, the survivors of a sea battle with the Spanish in 1568? I imagined a great compression of time, and in that compression, the Spanish chasing the English chasing the Spanish chasing the French, like some mad animal chasing its tail: León after La Salle—the Spanish Fleet after Ingram, et al—and Piñeda, blithely sailing by and mumbling

Corpus Christi—all the while the indigenous Karankawa Indians, later to be called "Water-Walkers" because of their ability
to cross unseen shallow reefs and shifting sand bars on foot,
stood by and watched the carnival at a distance.

Although I was only a boy, as near as I could tell, Piñeda
had named the thing I came to know: *Corpus*. And I cursed
Piñeda for discovering this old Corpus. And while I felt no
urgent need to quest for other legendary lands in the New
Spanish World—such as the Fountain of Youth—it seemed
entirely reasonable to me that I should be questing or con-
quering or discovering—something. Were not these
men—these explorers—the standard bearers for generations
to come? And should not I somehow follow in their footsteps?
Should not I be on one knee, somewhere, claiming something
in the name of someone? But how, with so many explorers
before me, could I hope to be sure I would be the first to discover whatever it was I discovered? Of course, it occurred to
me that my ancestor Francisco Durante was not a conquistador at all, which in itself was only part of my greatest dread:
was it possible that my intellectual training and Eva's late
attention to my manners would amount to nothing? She read
the Chivalric Code to me nights before bed, parts of which
impressed me little: all the trouble over women and being
smitten by them. We began *Don Quijote*, very slow, but I did
my best to stay with it, especially since Eva spoke of the old
book with such reverence... *El Quijote*, she called it, the *One
and Only*. She also made me recite verse in Latin from grandfather Francisco's primer of the same. All this I felt would be
wasted if the legend of my ancestor were not true: a whole
year of conquistador training down the drain.

One morning, I sat in the kitchen and watched Eva chop
tomatoes, corn, chicken, and beans and drop them with her
tiny hands into her pot for her *olla podrida*. I asked her:

"What kind of conquistador am I? I'm bored. What should
I *do*?"

She wiped the backs of her hands on her apron. "You will be what you will be—it's your destiny."

And so we pressed on with my training. I completed my introduction to Latin by reciting, to Eva's adoring satisfaction, the epigraph to Wordsworth's "Ode to Duty," one of grandfather Francisco's favorites:

Jam non consilio bonus, sed more eo
perductus, ut non tantum recte
facere possim, sed nisi recte
facere non possim...

Now at last I am not consciously good
but so trained by habit that I not only
can act rightly but cannot act
otherwise than rightly...

I thought the epigraph was perfect, and since I had memorized it so carefully, I felt I knew its profound and yet simple meaning. During that year I came to believe I could not do anything wrong—that the habits of a trained conquistador could not be anything but feared and admired by the worlds of less fortunate people. I could not, I believed, act unless it was right—so I decided to run away—rather, to *quest* for what I began to believe was my *destiny*—a strange word, and vague idea. I thought, I would be who I would be. Well, then, I would be a runaway, thereby seeking and finding at the same time, as I understood the concept, my *destiny*.

While Eva was feeding her chickens I went to her room and broke into her Francisco's chest, knowing I would find his First World War clothes. I put them on, found his dull, rusty bayonet, and tried on his wide-brimmed iron helmet, but it kept slipping front to back over my eyes and off my head, down my back and onto the floor. So I left it.

I rolled up the sleeves and pant legs of Francisco's gray musty-smelling war clothes and struck out for Corpus Christi Bay and the Gulf of Mexico. The sun was low on the horizon, changing from white to yellow over the ocean; an orange corona hugged it at last, and mobs of clouds clumped around it like purple grapes. As I approached the beach, the sky was dark, and the wind strong against my face. I sat for a long while near the beach with Francisco's bayonet across my knees. I could hear the long ragged fronds of a palm tree rattling together above me. Then I walked out to the beach, this time south of the breakwater. There, I decided to strike south, to walk the coast to South America.

The tide was in, and at the line of surf that pushed thin sheets of water to my feet were clumps of sea moss, and yellow, black, and red ropy strands of weed, among which lay several Portuguese men-of-war with their long, dark, tapered stingers tangled in the weed, and their gelatinous, pale-blue sails poking up. Further ahead of me, ghost crabs zigzagged among humps of weed and men-of-war, always just beyond the full range of human sight—beyond absolute, positive identification. That I felt I knew they were ghosts came only with experience, and with a kind of faith in the existence of creatures who live just out of light's reach. I was not far south of the breakwater, when I came to a small tidal pool with a few blades of grass standing out of it.... Suddenly, dozens of fiddler crabs were at my feet, holding their absurd little lances high, tacking sideways with me as I walked, their eyes like tiny black beads dead on me. I was enraged at the stupid little creatures, and I struck at them with Francisco's bayonet. I tipped them over one by one and, when I could slow one enough with the blade, jabbed the bayonet into its underside.

I felt an odd, frightening, yet uncontrollable need to kill, and kill, and keep killing, followed by the voice I'd heard inside me before: *perhaps*, I thought, then, *not yet, not yet*, then, *perhaps I am*, but I grew more and more distracted by the need to kill the fiddlers and by their legs, quivering and moving in circles as they struggled to right themselves.

The helpless gear-like workings of their legs amazed me more and more, and I slaughtered dozens of them—before I spotted the headlights of Francisco's Falcon parked near the breakwater behind me, then Eva, stooping and falling to her knees, then rising and crawling down the rocks toward me. I threw the bayonet down and ran; I twisted my ankle; I crawled and stumbled as fast as I could, yet Eva managed to tackle me, haul me up and—miraculously—lift me in her arms.

"Don't touch me!" I screamed with my face in my hands. "Don't look at me! I am a conquistador!"

I said this to her over and over—I am never sure if Eva responded in any way to my commands. I do know I was amazed all the while at the old woman's strength as she crawled up the rocks of the breakwater with me in her arms to Francisco's Falcon.

She let me go when we reached the car. I stood by the bumper on one leg and rubbed my ankle.

"You are a conquistador," Eva said, panting. "You are also a bad little boy."

"But my destiny!" I reproached, and she smiled a moment which calmed me—I was sure my esteemed ancestry had gotten me out of another bind.

Then she said, "It is your destiny, little boy, to be spanked and to spend tomorrow in your room."

I have carried the humiliation of Eva's hand to my bare backside all these years—yet I never whimpered once—stroke after stroke of her hand—sting after sting until the pain fairly glowed in my lower body. But I never whimpered, and I have never asked to this day how Eva might have felt about the humiliation she so passionately put upon her conquistador, the grandson of Francisco Durante—and I shall never know. I do know from that day on I was utterly alone in whatever quest destiny might throw my way...

By the grace of God, and I know it must have been by His grace alone, I graduated high school, happy to have the uneasy days living with Eva after my humiliation behind me. But that seemed to be the extent of His guiding hand. I joined the Navy in 1971 and was assigned duty on a destroyer. But I soon spent six months in the brig for slugging an Army sergeant who said sailors sail, soldiers fight. I expect I showed him the difference. When I got out of the brig, I saw many places and the people in them: the stony outlines of people at Pompeii, the Pyramids and their regal sarcophagi in the tombs of the Pharaohs, the temples of Montezuma, the stone steps leading to sacrificial altars; yet never in my travels did I ever quest for one thing; never did my destiny speak to me to say *this way* or *that way*; still, like the wilder days of my youth, other voices, such as those a wanderer is wont to hear, rose in me aboard ship as I lay awake nights with the diesels humming: *not yet, not yet, not yet* ... followed by silence and my utter dread of my heritage, the dark idea of it all, that my true self lay buried and shifting in the watery catacombs of the Gulf.

Eva died in her little tar-papered house in Corpus while I was on duty at sea, aboard my destroyer, and I'll never know precisely where I was or what my thoughts were when she passed away. I returned to Corpus Christi—a short leave granted only for that purpose—to settle her affairs. As I remember, after the funeral, I came upon the tiny white house suddenly, and as I turned the steering wheel quickly left to enter the crushed seashell drive, my only thought was to find Francisco's chest, and to save his possessions from the last rites of surveyor, bank, and land agent. I entered through the front of the house and came to the room—Francisco's, and Eva's room for the years after his passing—where I knew his chest rested, but I heard again the propellers of my destroyer moaning in my ears, *not yet*. So I turned from Francisco's room, and went straight down the hall, past the kitchen, and into the back yard, where three chickens still paced Eva's coop. I tossed them some corn from the coffee can nailed near the gate, then stood there awhile watching them take up the

corn, and hearing, I imagined, the fiddlers around me scratch-
ing over the sand, and the same voice again I had heard all
the years since I left Eva, and the memory of Francisco
Durante, and my humiliation...*not now...not now...not
here*...

I turned and went back to the house, through the wooden
screen door and into Eva's kitchen. There, all in a single
square of light thrown from the narrow window over the sink,
where the worried surfaces of a stone pot and platter, where
three wooden spoons and the cans of pintos and chicken bones
for crabbing at the breakwater rested—there, I named her—
mi abuela, my Eva—there, and not on the silent slopes of
Darien overlooking the Pacific, not in the prison of night
where the naked palms shake against the sky, or in the dark,
shifting bottom of the Gulf that so stubbornly kept the bones
of my ancestors—there, where by the small table in the center
of the kitchen I lowered myself to one knee.

El Centauro del Norte

About half of what I will tell you is true. I do not say this because I am a liar, or because I believe history is a bad dream. Rather, I say this because I believe there are other halves of the story buried in the story, halves of the story that are also true—halves that perhaps spring from a side of me, my family, the speakers of *los cuentos*, that are curiously not buried in shadows, not dark halves that hide their faces from the public, but halves that bare their little faces to the light, so open and pure in their telling from each tongue that all their little faces become true themselves, half-truths of all things...but everyone knows, as mathematicians tell us now, that too many halves, no matter how true, never become whole...

But in my family there exists one great story made of more halves than will fit into it. No matter where we have been, or gone, or go, the story is passed on, and in my fifteenth year it was given to me, first by my grandfather Mariano Luis Guzmán, not immediately, but after the prompting of my mother, Gloria.

One bright June day, I found Gloria in her kitchen, where we lived in Cleveland, Ohio, cupping her hands around some crumbs from breakfast on the table. She herded the crumbs into a little heap, and said, "When we are in Corpus Christi, you ask your grandfather Mariano about El Centauro del Norte. He will tell you the story."

I moved over to the table, near Gloria, and watched as she swept the heap of crumbs into the upturned palm of one hand

and carried them to the sink. She made a little wave with her hand and scattered the crumbs into the drain.

"What is this story?"

"No," she said. "You wait—he'll tell you himself."

Before that moment with Gloria and her little handful of crumbs, I grew up thinking, now only guessing, that my family's great story was that of my father, Martín Guzmán, who after working in the cotton fields outside Corpus, having only, as Gloria tells it, saltines sopped in milk for breakfasts and lunches, joined the Navy, was stationed at Corpus Christi, toured in Korea while I was born, returned to haul pipe string into West Texas, near Lubbock, then attended the University of Texas at Austin on the GI Bill and, remarkably, graduated with honors in nuclear physics. He took us, regretfully, but with great determination and hope for the future, into the north of the country, to a faraway place called Cleveland, where he worked for NASA at the Lewis Research Center.

This had been the greatest story I had ever known—that such a man and his family might have made such a quantum leap from life in the fields, over a kind of high and rocky watershed dividing north and south, time before and after the Korean War, while in Corpus so many others remained as my grandfather Mariano did now—closer to cotton than physics and deep-space travel.

Though we lived so far from Corpus, we visited Mariano with each vacation the government granted Father, three weeks, which he sometimes took, two in Corpus, one at Niagara Falls. And I looked forward to visiting Mariano, especially since he would take me to the Serpentine Wall, and its breakwater running out, made of large white irregularly-shaped boulders snaking far into Corpus Christi Bay and the Gulf of Mexico. It was wonderful to walk along the wall, the idea of it, the experience of extending myself so far out into the wide sea simply by walking, or crawling onto the winding rocks, by travel in a familiar way.

There, on the wall, a speck in the endless blue of sky and sea, I'd carry two buckets, balancing myself carefully as I followed Mariano. One bucket was empty for the blue crabs we'd catch, the other full of chicken bones Mariano had saved for crabbing. Later, as we made our way far out onto the wall and into the bay, the sky seemed half bare—a sheet of low clouds stretched like linen over the ocean, then broke in a ragged line behind us near the beach. Inland, over my birth city, the noon sun showered light.

I followed Mariano, though awkwardly, zigzagging over the top of the sea wall, half my mind on the unfathomable expanse of water in the Gulf, the other half on the stiff sea air in my face. I was so distracted I fell behind Mariano, so I ran a few steps, skipping, the pails knocking my knees, to catch up with him. Mariano walked in his slow deliberate way, the brim of his straw stetson broken across the front, little bits of straw sticking out along the break. The broken brim was pulled down, shading his eyes and dividing his face into patches of light and dark. I could see the brownish band of sweat along the bowl of the hat—an ancient sweat, there as long as I could remember, a kind of unique human hieroglyph for toil under the sun. It ran up from the base of the hat where it met the back of his neck in a mark like a small hand with its fingers closed. His face was long, his forehead high, and I found it remarkable that he had all his teeth. In fact, when he turned to be sure I was following him with the buckets, he smiled, and I was sure his teeth were perfect, so perfect that I wondered if they were real...but that was not what I needed to find out, so when we settled on a couple rocks, tied some bones to our lines, and tossed them out, I asked him, as Gloria had told me I should, "Tell me about El Centauro del Norte."

I saw one eye of his in the shade of the straw stetson; he rubbed his chin, pulled a couple times on his line with a finger, wishing, it seemed, that a crab would take the bone so he could delay his response...perhaps...but I believe the best of him, even now, and believe in that pause and tiny tug at the line, Mariano was sizing me up to see if I was old enough to hear the story. So I rubbed my chin back at him, saw him smile a bit at one corner of his mouth, and again saw his perfect teeth, which may have been false...

"All right," he said, "you see, I didn't want to be a U.S. citizen; this all happened when I lived in Puerto Rico. My parents worked on a tobacco plantation there. When I was born, I was a citizen of Puerto Rico and Spain, then after the War with America, the island became a territory of the United States—and my parents told me we belonged to the United States. But all the time I did not care much about it. I was a boy, and things, as far as I could see, were the same. I worked with my father in the drying house, and my new country, the United States, was nothing—I was in Puerto Rico—see? Well, I was small and could climb like a monkey. So my father would load my arms and shoulders with tobacco leaves until I'd look like a little tobacco king with broad green leaves for sleeves and a coat with green tails. Then I'd climb the slats in the drying house." Mariano gestured at the sky with the flat of one hand, "*Zip*—you see? And I would drape the leaves on the rafters high in the top of the house. My father would hang the leaves on the lower slats. This was how I was in those days. The work was hard and hot, but I never minded because I was like a monkey—see?

"But then, in 1915, my father said I must join the army of the United States. 'What?' I said to my father. 'Why do I have to go?' My father folded his arms over his chest and said, 'It is your duty.'" Mariano took his line in the two first fingers of his right hand and gave it a little yank. I saw him start to turn to me, to see my reaction to his story so far, but I turned away before he could look. Somehow, I knew if I showed him I was indifferent, I'd draw more of the story out of him, and he continued, "You see, I was like a monkey and a boy, a Puerto Rican and an American—soldier, tobacco hanger—I was suddenly all these things, when all I wanted to be was a monkey with tobacco on his back who worked with his father in the great, high, airy, sweet-smelling drying house.

"So, in obedience to my father, I left my home, sad and desperate, not worried about fighting the Hun in Europe, or dying, only wondering how someday I would get back home. I did not want to belong to the United States if it meant leaving my home...but I went to the dock and took a ship with other boys to New York, where I was made into a soldier in the Fifth Infantry, the Fighting Red Devils of New York." The sun had gone over the midpoint of the sky, drawing a little line of shade made by Mariano's stetson closer to his eyes, nearly revealing both eyes, so he paused a moment in telling his story, glanced at the sun, and tugged the brim downward to shade his face. "I made friends in New York in the Fighting Red Devils," he said, "and I became a little happy about that, but I never forgot about my home, and some nights I would stay awake all night wondering about my family in Puerto Rico, then, dozing in the very early morning before the bugle sounded, I would dream of the tobacco house and the smell of the leaves and climbing high into its rafters...

"Instead of sending us to Europe, in 1916 we were ordered to go to Texas; so we took a train to El Paso. I was surprised by this since I never thought I would have a chance of going anywhere south again, nearer to my home. There, in El Paso, we marched and practiced shooting our guns over and over, until one day we were ordered to go to Eagle Pass. So we marched southeast along the Rio Grande to Eagle Pass, just across el Rio from Piedras Negras—and after about ten days, we set up camp outside the town.

"At first, I didn't know why we were there—no one did—or if they did, my English was so bad I didn't know any-one was talking about it. But I was getting tired of all this practicing, and was homesick, until one of my friends said to me, very slowly, 'Mariano, you'll appreciate this.... We are going after Pancho Villa.' 'Pancho Villa?' I thought. He didn't mean anything to me. I couldn't figure why so many soldiers had come so far to get just one man. For this I had to leave my home? My family?

"When we had been in Eagle Pass about a week, we were given a day's leave. The other boys went into town to the cantinas, but I just wandered around the town, going nowhere, thinking nothing, I was so homesick—can you imagine this?" I saw the skin around Mariano's lips and his crabbing line tighten at the same time—he seemed grateful for the little pull on his line, because, again, he didn't seem to want to go on with the story. He brought the crab in hand over hand, out of the water. A couple of times the crab smacked against a rock then swung side to side in the air on the line, still clamping its chela on the chicken bone—and I wondered that moment what must have possessed the little crustacean to hang onto the tiny bone, despite its being hauled out of its natural element. Hunger? Stubbornness? And again I looked at the sky, feigning boyish indifference to Mariano's story, and noticing that the line of clouds over the bay and city had been pushed back, out to sea, by the high sun.... Mariano quickly stripped the crab from his line, dropped it into the pail, and continued, "I walked awhile west of Eagle Pass, El Paso del Aquila, until I came to a settlement of small houses and many tents inhabited by *los colonizadores*, a place called La Colonia. I came to a little ravine cut square by a storm that wound off to the south and, I imagined, drained into the Rio Grande. There, near a little pile of dark rocks across the ravine, I saw a rider on a gray horse, with long bullets in ammunition belts crossing his chest, a thick high sombrero, a long thin rifle lashed to his saddle. He wore a gray canvas jacket and leathery *pantalones*. But all his clothes were blended together in the distance, blended even more with the snakes of heat rising from the ground...

"All of a sudden the rider kicked his horse and started across the ravine. I stood where I was. I didn't move. Where could I go? But even as the rider came closer, he seemed so

stiff and straight in the saddle, and his gear so hard and
bleached all the same color by the sun, that he looked as if he
were a part of his horse, part of the same animal—a man and
animal himself, together, coming at me, beating the ground
with four feet, coming at me...

"When he rode up to me and reined in his horse, I saw
only one thing new, his thick, black mustache that covered his
upper lip. His mustache was shaggy like a dog's hair." Mariano ran a finger over his lip. "See, *muchacho*?... Well, the
rider held the reins stiffly in one hand, and he had his other
hand near the stock of his rifle. I remember the vein sticking
out of the hand by the rifle. He didn't seem to want to say anything, and I was sure, then, that this man and his horse were
going to kill me, so I blurted out, 'What are you?' He shifted in
his saddle a bit and I heard the leather creaking, which
relieved me at the moment, but he never moved his hand with
the big vein from his rifle. 'Don't you know?' he said. 'You've
been looking for me.' 'Me?' I said. 'No...I haven't been looking
for you, *señor*. I don't know what you mean. I'm not looking for
you.' Then a thought formed in my mind, a silly thought, the
thought that this rude ammo-belted man was Pancho
Villa—right? But where was his army? Where were his Red
Flaggers, his *soldaderas*, the *Yaqui*...all the people's armies
my friends in the Fighting Red Devils had told me about? The
Brothers of La Cucaracha, *Las Cucarachas*, humble, ugly, and
indestructible, like the song, song of the common soldier...
Muchacho," Mariano said to me, "this is the song I'm telling
you about," and he began to sing, first in Spanish, then English:

> La cucaracha, la cucaracha
> Ya no puede caminar;
> Porque no tiene, porque le falta,
> Marihuana que fumar.
>
> Una vieja y un viejito,
> se cayeron en un pozo;

Y la vieja dijo al viejo:
¡Viejito tan asqueroso!

La cucaracha, la cucaracha...

The *cucaracha*, the *cucaracha*,
He won't travel anymore;
Because he hasn't, because he's lacking
Marihuana left to smoke.

Once a *viejo* and a *vieja*,
fell into an empty well;
Said the *vieja* to the *viejo*:
Dirty old man go to hell!

The *cucaracha*, the *cucaracha*...

Mariano hummed a few more bars of the song and took in another crab, then he said, "But I want to tell you if this man shot me, all right?" I nodded and he continued, "So the man on the horse said, 'I am El Centauro del Norte...' and I said, 'So you are Pancho Villa?' and he said, shifting again in his saddle, 'Don't interrupt me or I will kill you—see?' So I said nothing and he said, 'I am El Centauro.... While your Twelfth Cavalry is looking for me at Boca Chica, I am here looking at *you*!... And so you have found me. Now, what do you want?' I didn't know what I wanted, but I thought I'd better think of something fast, so I said, 'General Villa, I just want to go back to Puerto Rico and work with my father in the tobacco house.' Then he laughed: he removed his big sombrero with one hand and nearly doubled over, laughing in his saddle. Then as he laughed I saw him draw his hand with the big vein sticking out away from his rifle. I saw my chance, so I ran. I ran without looking back, remembering his sombrero waving in the air, and hearing only his laughter.

"That night, back with the Fighting Red Devils outside Eagle Pass, I lay awake a long time, very late, wondering if I should tell anyone about seeing General Villa near La Colonia—but I didn't, thinking how I might have to tell them also what I had said to him about my wish to go home—and I couldn't, you see, think of any words to substitute for my homesickness, or a way to speak them without feeling humiliated when I recalled General Villa's laughter and his sombrero waving at me as I ran..."

It didn't seem to bother Mariano that I hadn't any questions for him about his story, questions he might have expected a fifteen-year old to ask. Mariano's story silenced me. It was beyond me to look back a generation, two generations, across the mélange of facts and to imagine that Mariano of the broken straw brim, Mariano of the shaded eyes, was once a monkey in a sweet-smelling tobacco house. As unfathomable was that he had met a man my history teacher had characterized as "that bandit of the Revolution." What was within my reach was that Mariano had been homesick—we all were in our own ways—Gloria for her family in San Antonio, that we visited on a two-day trip; Mariano for his wife, Pilar, then dead five years; Father for his mother, Pilar; and Father for Mariano, knowing he'd brought his young family so far north to leave Mariano in Corpus with his stories, small house, and chicken coop on Old Brownsville Road. So our yearly reunion was not a reunion at all, but a kind of silent lamentation of many generations. We ate, we laughed, then came the time to be silent—and I was, in this silence, over and over, dispatched from Father to Mother, from Mother to Grandfather, and more, to hear all their stories separately, my special sort of loneliness, hearing each half coming out and growing in my mind like so many ragged fronds of the palms of Corpus that rattled in the hot wind saying many things at once, meaning none...

Later that afternoon, after Mariano and I returned from crabbing near the Serpentine Wall, I saw Father in the driveway. He was pulling spark plugs from Mariano's little old

Comet sedan. The car was a vague color of green, faded from the sun, baked out as it had stood years in the heat of the light reflected by bright white bits of seashells filling the driveway.

I said to Father, "Mariano told me about El Centauro del Norte when we were crabbing."

"He did? Well, then he must have told you about how he joined the Revolution. He was a wagoner under Orestes Pereyra near Piedras Negras."

"No," I said, then added politely, "maybe he was, but he didn't tell me."

"You see," Father said, "Mariano met General Villa outside Eagle Pass—this was maybe 1915 or 1916, I don't know..."

"Yes, I know."

"Good, well, General Villa said to Mariano, 'Do you want to join the Brotherhood of the Cockroaches?' And your grandfather replied, 'Yes, I am going home to Puerto Rico, and if I can go back there after the Revolution is won, I'll be most grateful,' and so the Centaur reached his hand down to Mariano and took him up behind him on his horse, and they made swiftly across the Rio Grande for Piedras Negras."

This certainly puzzled me, so I said to Father, "He didn't say anything about Pereyra or fighting with Pancho Villa."

"He didn't?..." Father said, leaning into the engine of the car, his torso disappearing behind the engine block. "I wonder why not.... That silly old man, leaving things out, making stories all the time—you never know what to believe."

"Then the part about meeting the Centaur—that may not be true?"

Father suddenly stood up, out of the engine, and looked at me sternly.

"Yes, of course. That part is true. Everybody knows that! Ask your mother!"

I left Father wiping a spark plug with a greasy rag. I went to Mariano's chicken coop and sat by it to ponder this new part of Mariano's story. I suspected, watching three chickens peck the corn scattered in one corner of the coop, that Mariano had not told me the real story because he still feared being labeled a deserter from the army, or worse, a traitor to the United States. Still, he had apparently told Father about his traitorous act, and now I knew as well, but I somehow felt nervous knowing this about the Monkey Boy, about my own kind, about being traitors to the United States, so I found Gloria in what had been Pilar's kitchen. She stood by the tiny window at the back of the kitchen; her elbows rested on a narrow windowsill, and her chin rested in her palms. She stared out the window at what appeared to be the spot near the chicken coop where I had been sitting moments before—but I was there, behind her, so it may have been another place she was staring at—or through—or, it seemed at the time, beyond.

"Mama," I said, and she turned her head slightly without removing her elbows from the sill, or her chin cradled in her palms. "Father told me to ask you about when Mariano rode with General Villa and Pereyra, near Piedras Negras."

"What?" she whispered, then louder, "What?... That crazy *Viejito*! He would not have ridden with Villa—and *General* Villa? *General*? My foot! That butcher, that disgusting womanizing brute—El Centauro del Norte... *Sí*, that's what he was—looked like a man, acted like some *animal*." She turned around and leaned with her back on the windowsill, propping herself slightly away from it by putting her arms behind her. "Let me tell you about Mariano. He was a deserter. He got so homesick for Puerto Rico he just walked right out of the camp at Eagle Pass. Some Fighting Red Devil. But I can't say I blame him...*estúpido Estados Unidos*...*estúpido castrense*...but he was so homesick, right, that he walked straight out of the army camp and headed for Puerto Rico, all on his own, with nothing!"

"So he never had a leave and never joined the Brotherhood of the Cockroaches and fought with Pereyra for Villa?"

"*Sí*, never. Your grandfather was just a homesick little boy. That's all. He wanted to go home, but he only made it as far as Corpus Christi. He was hungry, starving. He never went home."

Finally, I felt the tremor of certainty, so I struck home.

"And Villa...he never met the Centaur?"

"*Pues*...of course he did! But that's not the point!"

So, disappointed that none of the stories seemed to match, I asked myself, what *was* the point? Mariano himself had told me that he was many things at once, monkey boy, soldier...but could all of these incongruous things also exist in one person's life? How could they? So I made my mind up to work on the puzzle, and I went to walk along Old Brownsville Road, out the porch and west past Villarreal's Lounge. After walking a short time, I found an old horseshoe in the dust and shells, bits of broken, weathered asphalt covering the berm of the road. I passed a patch of prickly pear. I looked at the sky, gone orange in its corners, where two clouds, each shaped like a 'C,' hugged the fat sun on each side. I stopped to watch a trail of fire ants cross my shoe, not afraid of them, but fascinated by them.... My skin pimpled, even in the heat, and I had the strangest sensation...that if horseshoes and clouds shaped like 'C's' and fire ants and prickly pears could all exist the moment of my little walk, then... What?... Could these stories? If one ant in the entire trail across the toe of my shoe was merely a phantom, does it somehow render all ants in all ant trails, all horseshoes and strangely formed clouds under heaven—all needles in the pale, green flesh of the prickly pear false? Perhaps not...perhaps that was it, why the story in all its versions seemed so important and true and vital to Mariano and Martin and Gloria—that is, for each needle in the prickly pear that is untrue, several others no doubt will be there to remind you of their painful validity. So I sensed that all the stories could, in the most outrageous way, be true—Mariano running from Villa, joining Villa, or deserting the Fighting Red Devils—all of it, since my crazy mama and papa and *abuelo* all persisted in their belief of the Centaur, and there, standing with my horseshoe by the prickly pear and trail of ants, I first felt a strange kind of logic—that if one believed one great story, then all the other halves of it, no matter how inconsistent, so long as they were part of the great story, could also, in a way, be believed.

But on my way back to the house, the night came on, the air stirred and washed over me in little waves against my skin, and there in the strong dark night at the side of Old Brownsville Road I lost something, my nerve, my vision. And when I came to the stoop outside Mariano's house, I again felt my old need to verify just one part of his story, the part about the Centaur. I wanted to believe in more than books say. I wanted to know that such a meeting with Villa had taken place and that, then, all meetings of all people in history could be possible, true, significant.

When I came in the front door, to my left a single lamp burned over Mariano. He was sleeping and snoring, making growling sounds that came from deep inside his sinuses. He had pulled both his legs up to his chest, and he lay curled like a little animal in the chair. He wore his shirt, but had removed his pants, and his thin legs, peppered with gray hair, reminded me how, still, he was a monkey boy, and took me outside myself, to the high rafters of the tobacco house in Puerto Rico he had never returned to. I could almost smell it...and that moment I knew that even if nothing else were true, I believed, I lived, deeply and precisely, in Mariano's tobacco house.

I put out the light and, watching him sleep so well, felt a little ashamed for wanting to ask him once more about El Centauro del Norte.

In a few days we prepared to leave Corpus, and I prepared for the worst sorts of good-byes. But this time, this visit, Mariano decided to leave his tiny house on Old Brownsville Road to come live with us in Cleveland. Three days in our car, two motels, across the Mississippi, then the Ohio, Mariano was quiet, and I felt his silence inside myself, felt his silence silence me...

Home for a time, a few weeks, having Mariano in our house in Cleveland, sitting in our yellow, webbed, aluminum lawn chair at one corner of our yard, or in our kitchen with his coffee, seemed exciting. And Mariano, too, was curious about the small things we had discovered in the north of America, the things that became part of our lives—our garbage disposal, our dimming light switches, clean and full plazas and strips of jazzy stores. But after a time I could feel his homesickness for Corpus, for Puerto Rico, as I had felt his silence in myself during the trip North; and I became in an uncertain way homesick myself feeling his loss.... But there were times, nights when Father and Gloria would fill the cooler with ice and stab bottles of beer by their bottoms into it, and bring the cooler to the patio, set it dead center there, then light great oil torches at all sides, and join Mariano sitting in his little yellow chair so far from home to make *los cuentos*, our little stories whose many halves I grew to know were true, grew to believe, and came to know my half, hearing time to time one of my parents or Mariano say, and make a little laugh, *You've been looking for me.... What do you want?* or, *Do you want to join the Brotherhood of the Cockroaches? The Revolution?*

I grew to know my half hearing their little halves, seeing their little faces in the light of the great torches, my half in my face in that same light when, afterward, I was alone and the light of torches doused, and I'd find my horseshoe from Old Brownsville Road, imagine with the exactness of dreams I had grown four legs, straight and strong, and wandered with them through the black rocks of the Rio, looking, looking...and why not? All stories are true, no matter how brutish or beautiful, and though we had come very far from the land of our dreams, though each of us in some tiny, fractured way would always be homesick, our homesickness was part of the story too, part of the story made of each one of our many halves, of the story we each held as our own, but part of someone else's story too, part of some long-forgotten whole.

The Banker's Son

The houses are haunted
By white night-gowns.
None are green,
Or purple with green rings,
Or green with yellow rings,
Or yellow with blue rings.
None of them are strange...

—Wallace Stevens,
"Disillusionment of Ten O'Clock"

Eolo had two kinds of recollections about his early child-hood. One sort were his easy recollections. Among these was his knowledge that he had a father he met when he was too young to remember, that this father never lived with him or his mother, and that this father was somehow hopelessly lost. Eolo might pass this father on the steamy streets of Corpus Christi, Texas, and never recognize him. His mother, Casandra, described this father freely: he was a young man of Dutch descent, a banker's son, with a pale square face, a broad jutting chin, stiff bristly light hair, and closely set blue eyes. Eolo also discovered that his father, like his father before him, had become a banker.

Eolo took many of his features from this father, in fact, all, except that Eolo's hair was limp and dark brown, and his eyes like two black pearls. So Eolo often stared at the blue-eyed men who walked the plazas in the center of town or the expanses of concrete skirting the great sea wall with its steps leading directly to the water of Corpus Christi Bay. He

wondered at their gray suits and ten-gallon velvet hats, yet as
he did, he noticed how many of them grew uncomfortable with
his stare. They rubbed their hands and looked away. They
glanced nervously at their wristwatches. They removed their
hats, stared at the headbands inside, turned them over and
over in their hands, then replaced them on their heads.

As a child, Eolo flattered himself into believing that all
the blue-eyed cowboy businessmen had something to hide,
that any of them might be this father of his, or that each of
them had a son like him that they had abandoned: his mother
explained to him that this father of his left them because this
father's father told him to do so. She explained to Eolo that his
father was a good son and had obeyed his father. Eolo found
this to be ironic. He would never be a good son, he reasoned,
while turning these easy recollections around in his mind: to
whom should he show obedience?

While it was easy for Eolo to recall his first ideas about
this father, his first recollections of his mother were more difficult. Certainly, there were the usual facts he came to possess
about her: Casandra was the daughter of a Mexican couple
who crossed the Rio Grande from Piedras Negras to Eagle
Pass in 1932. The couple settled in Corpus Christi and the
husband painted signs for a living. Casandra attended a
Catholic school, where she learned English and catechism.
She finished two years of college before she was pregnant with
Eolo. So Eolo's features resulted from these particulars about
his lineage: he was part Dutch and part Mexican.

But unlike his father, whichever father it may have been
crossing plazas of Corpus Christi, his mother was also a
source of wonder. Casandra was a diminutive woman, and he
could not get past this fact when he considered the particulars
of how she might have given him birth. He had come from
such a small woman. He had issued from such a tiny, beautiful woman with olive skin, a slight nose, and short, limp black
hair. It was as if he came from some place so miniscule that it
seemed to him no place at all. He was amazed at his very exis-

tence, and it was this, knowing the source of his birth, seeing her each day, yet not believing she could have given him life, that made him uneasy.

After Eolo was born, Casandra and he lived ten years with her parents at their house on Old Brownsville Road: a narrow broken asphalt strip running west to east into town. When he was eleven, his mother rented a small single-story house with shingle siding and a tar-paper roof several miles west of the grandparents' house on Old Brownsville Road. She saved the deposit and first month's rent with a little money she earned cleaning fish and a larger sum borrowed from her parents.

To Eolo, the house seemed like a concoction of shapes and colors. The siding shingles were different shades of white and green and brown. The tar paper on the roof was checkered with several fresh, black strips—and many older, weathered strips that were a dead-gray color. Three persimmon trees covered the eastern wall of the house, and vines of morning glory extended from the trees and spiraled over a white wooden trellis that spanned the narrow gravel drive. He greatly admired the arch in the trellis over the drive, the papery lavender flowers, and the persimmons, but a large garden spider—with black and irregular yellow markings—had made a web in the arch of the trellis, and Eolo refused to pass under it. When he pointed to the spider, which never seemed to budge from its position in the center of the web, Casandra quickly hustled him around one side or the other of the trellis, uncustomarily cursing to herself in Spanish.

It was in this house that Eolo had another uneasy recollection: late one night, a white scorpion picked its way up the screen in his bedroom window, its plated underside luminescent in the moonlight. The hot, wet air ran through the screen, over his hands and across his face as he lay waiting in the way he waited most nights for sleep to overcome him. Then sleep came—a dark, wet sleep—and the feeling of a coolness traveling his face. He woke suddenly to find Casandra kneeling beside his bed. She pressed a cold egg to his cheek. She did not look at him. She focused on the egg as she rolled it along the line of his jaw and down onto his neck. Eolo lay very still. When the egg began to grow warm, he closed his eyes, and Casandra withdrew it from his face. When he reopened his eyes, she left the room and went back to hers across the hall. The scorpion had disappeared from the screen, and the air remained damp and still.

Later that same evening, Eolo woke again and heard someone knocking at the front door. He waited to hear Casandra rise to answer the door. But the knocking stopped, and he believed she had not stirred in her room.

The next day, he did not ask Casandra about the egg or the knocking at the door. The egg had been cool and refreshing on his face, and in fact he slept better afterward. The knocking had stopped so suddenly, simultaneously with his waking to it, that it seemed too altogether dream-like to be worth mentioning.

He spent most of the day at his grandparents' house while Casandra worked. There, about noon, he found an egg in the icebox and rolled it over his face and neck. His grandmother took the egg from him and put it back into the icebox. He expected a scolding from her; instead, she looked at him calmly with her arms crossed, as if she were waiting for him to explain something she already knew. After a time her expression changed from a kind of serenity to one that seemed to Eolo regretful or sad. Then she found her husband in the living room, exchanged a few angry words with him, and returned to the kitchen to start dinner.

Eolo did not speak Spanish fluently. Casandra forbade him to use it with her, and she warned her parents not to use it with him, but he knew enough to understand what his grandparents usually bickered about: the grandfather wanted

Casandra to return to their home since they had been subsi-
dizing her rent payments all along. They were not well off, but
they managed. When his grandparents came to Corpus, they
had a difficult time, but when the war in Europe started, his
grandfather opened a small sheet-metal bending shop and
worked a few subcontract jobs at the shipyard. Still, the
expense of keeping Eolo and Casandra in their tar-papered
house was bleeding him: *estoy triste*, his grandfather lament-
ed, *me desangro*.

His grandmother prattled on.... She would just as soon
cut them both loose—entirely. Eolo suspected that she was
weary of caring for him during his summers off school, though
he was not sure from her tone and manner of speech that the
matter was all that simple. But what puzzled him most about
his grandparents were the words they exchanged following
the incident with the egg. Their voices were held low and soft.
Their words were indistinguishable from muddled human
sounds. The words were not language, not at all like the loud
angry chatter he heard time and time again. The sounds they
made, calm and serious, but reticent, were underscored with
sorrow.

When school started in August, Eolo pushed his grandparents
from his thoughts. He rarely visited them, perhaps only once a
month, when Casandra was scheduled to work a double shift
at the pier. He was not an intense student, but he was generally liked by the other children, something he felt grateful for.
He had seen too many times how the other children treated
Anselmo, a boy whose hair was burned off and who was horribly scarred on the right side of his face in a fire that began
mysteriously late at night as his family slept. The boys called
Anselmo the Phantom and taunted him. The girls made wide
circles around him and dropped their heads in what seemed to

Eolo a sign of a deep abiding shame, a directionless shame, an unreasoned shame that seemed to overcome them.

Casandra continued her ritual with the egg throughout the summer, and soon he simply pretended to sleep while she knelt at his bed. By the end of October, she stopped rolling the egg over him, and he reasoned that the nights were cool enough that she saw no need for it. Then about the end of November, he awoke one night, and through slits in his eyes saw her kneel by his bed with a small bottle of olive oil in her right hand. She poured a drop of the oil on the tip of her index finger and pressed it to his forehead. When she closed her eyes he opened his a little more, and he believed he saw her lips moving, parting slightly then pressing themselves together, though this in no way resembled speech, silent or otherwise. He made his eyes again into slits and felt her rub the olive oil over his forehead: she placed the palms of her hands gently in the center of his forehead and pressed them slowly outward over his temples. She repeated this several times, until the olive oil spread and soaked his skin. Then she took an egg from the floor and ran it back and forth—temple to temple—across his forehead. Later that same night he heard the knocking at the front door, but it stopped when he thought he heard Casandra outside his door in the hall.

He thought about his mother and her ritual while at school the next day—not thinking as one who tries to discover the reason for such behavior, but with a child's gradual sense of its importance, a sense that the ritual signified the kind of person he was, more than the kind of person she was. At the morning recess, he pondered the matter as he sat on the ground poking at a chameleon's tail as it rested in the low branches of a Crepe bush. The chameleon started along a branch then dashed away into a tangle of leafy twigs. Anselmo, the Phantom, suddenly appeared standing over him, awfully close, showing his huge strawberry colored patch of scar tissue. Eolo leaned back on his hands, and the Phantom screamed: "I heard your mama is *loco!—Lo!—co!*"

Then the Phantom ran off.

Eolo rose halfway to chase him, then fell back onto the ground. The face had been hideous, and this, together with what the Phantom had said, and what he knew was his mother's odd behavior, made it difficult for him to confront the disfigured boy.

During the afternoon recess he saw three boys gather around the Phantom: the scarred boy knelt on one knee in the dust and the three boys circled him, kicking at the dust with the toes of their shoes. The dust boiled and obscured the Phantom. He tucked his head onto his chest and covered his eyes with his forearms. The boys left, the dust settled, and Eolo went over to him.

"Who said that about my mama?"

The scarred boy did not budge, and Eolo heard him laugh between his crossed forearms.

"The men at the pier told my papa.... Everyone knows she's *loco*. Leave me alone."

Eolo watched Anselmo crouching in the dust with his arms crossed over his eyes, and Eolo promised himself he would never be shunned by others so horribly.

Old Brownsville Road ran along the western outskirts of Corpus Christi, past several pecan, watermelon, and cotton farms, to the Naval Base and Gulf of Mexico. Over the years, a small tourist trade developed, so local investors financed a motor hotel located between the house of Casandra and Eolo and that of the grandparents. A short time later, a shopping plaza was built around an HEB Market, and several small businesses moved in: Space Burgers, Telemundo Cable Channel 66, the Euro-Hair School, and others. A golf course and VA hospital were built. Old Brownsville Road was widened, bringing the berm of the road nearly to Eolo's doorstep. His grandparents sold their home to a developer since it stood in the way of an apartment complex. They moved to San Antonio, and finally into a condominium overlooking the River Walk, at a bend noted for its vibrant, scarlet azaleas and overhanging willows. They begged Casandra to allow them to take Eolo with them—in fact they asked for both daughter and grand-child to come with them to San Antonio. But they only asked once, and Casandra resisted in that moment. She explained that Eolo was now old enough to be left alone at home, or at a friend's place.

With time, there were many minimum-wage jobs up and down Old Brownsville Road, but Eolo's mother did not find one. She told Eolo she was not lucky, and he did not entirely believe her. He began to wonder if *loco* people were not lucky. So Casandra continued to clean fish more hours a week. She never complained about trying—and not finding—steady work, even when Eolo knew she knew other Mexican Ameri-cans who had gotten jobs at over a dozen fast-food places near-by. It was a great puzzle to him: the sudden bulldozing, the widening of the road, his grandparents moving, the paving of the land around his mother's house, and his mother's misfor-tune. He suddenly felt—as he never had—that the small tar-papered house was merely a bit of rubbish, destined in a short while to be swept away.

Through it all, Casandra's rituals grew in frequency, intensity, and complexity. She continued to dot his forehead with olive oil and roll the cold egg over his face, and she start-ed to shake a can of minced garlic around his bed. While the smell of the garlic was not particularly bothersome, the gritty, dirty feeling of the garlic on the soles of his feet was a source of embarrassment, somehow the same embarrassment he felt when he thought about their tiny house amid the new plazas, shopping areas and restaurants. At bedtime, she also brewed aniseed tea for him to drink. She fed him a spoonful of honey, and gave him a wedge of lemon to place in his mouth and to bite into until he could feel his top and bottom teeth meet, the muscles in his mouth grow taut, and the bitter juice rinse the honey away. This he protested, but she ignored his first complaint so completely, so innocently, he felt ashamed at the time to speak about it again.

During periods of time—sometimes weeks—the knocking at the front door he believed he heard ceased, and although he was grateful for this, it did not lessen his increasing curiosity about Casandra's behavior. What seemed to frighten him most was not the queerness of her actions, but that he had become so accustomed to them; together they seemed to feed one another: the honey was delightful, the lemon a bit hard to take, though it ultimately refreshed his mouth; the aniseed tea made him vaguely drowsy, and after a time he believed it helped him sleep, and he could not, in the long run, complain about the cool sensation of the egg as she moved it over his face. Although his mother did not sweep up the garlic until after he left for school, he grew accustomed to the fragrance, and, of course, learned to step over the garlic in the morning. He found that his senses began to change, and he started to accept the ritual and to ignore the developments on Old Brownsville Road: new odors of burnt diesel, fried foods, the sounds of cars rushing by day and night.

His mother now slept long into the day, sometimes past noon, and sometimes missed getting to work until after one p.m. One day he found her sitting up in her bed at just such an hour, and it occurred to Eolo to ask her about her strange rites, but a much larger question formed in his mind.

"Who is it knocking at our door?"

"Your father."

"Why can't we live with him? Why do we stay here?"

She stared at him a long while, and she yawned.

"Because it is all we have."

"Anselmo says you are *loco*—is that why we live by ourselves?"

She closed her eyes. She did not seem sad or regretful as he had expected. Her lips were together and made a perfect line; her hands rested one over another in her lap; a moment, he felt she had died. She seemed perfectly serene.

"It's all the same everywhere for you and me," she said, and suddenly opened her eyes. "It makes no difference if I am *loco* or not."

Eolo went to her window and looked out to the hot, busy road, past the plaza strip, to where the road appeared as a notch in the horizon—and beyond, to the Gulf where he imagined that the world somehow ended. Indeed, it looked all the same: *What if she is right?* he asked himself.

A few nights later, Eolo woke suddenly, for no particular reason. It may have been a fragment of the dream about the scorpion on the screen that suddenly turned bad, all too frightening. When he awoke, the wires of the screen in his window seemed to glow faintly. The glow rose and fell in intensity. He got out of bed, forgetting for a moment about the trail of garlic grounds. He stepped on them. His feet recoiled from the floor—one, then the other—and he stripped the coarse granules from one foot, then the other, with the palms of his hands. He moved slowly to the window, then he backed into the wall and inched his way along it, so he could have an angular view of the small yard beyond the screen. Casandra was standing a few feet outside his window. She was barefoot, with only a long sheer white gown to cover her nakedness, and she held a single candle with both hands. She did not appear to see him. Then he noticed that her eyes were closed, and her lips moved slightly, continuously as if she were praying. He turned and found his way back along the wall, stepped over the garlic, and lay awake in his bed. He watched the wires in the screen irradiate the candlelight a long while, and finally, after a long struggle, drifted to sleep, remembering as he drifted only that it was nearly morning and the wires in the screen had still glowed.

It was late the next day when Eolo woke and found Casandra in the front room sitting on the sofa. She was wearing her jeans, and had stuffed her nightgown into them. Her bare arms lay along her thighs. She stared straight ahead, expressionless. Eolo watched her perfect, unmoving profile a moment, then, as he moved in front of her, he realized that the left side of her face and neck were blotched with purple and yellow bruises.

"I have reached the point of breaking," his mother said without looking at him. She did not seem to speak to him, or anyone; she simply spoke, automatically, "I am sure I will be insane. I mean that nothing will be the same now. Remember that. Remember this moment. Nothing will ever be the same again."

She stared at the yellowed plaster wall across the room without blinking.

"Who did this?"

"Bud," she whispered. "Your father's name is Bud."

She rose from the sofa and walked out the front door. Eolo watched her walk slowly down Old Brownsville Road, east toward the Gulf. He did not follow her. He spent the rest of the day straightening the house. He made himself some aniseed tea, and during the hottest hour of the day he found a cold egg to rub on his face. Then he dozed most of the afternoon and evening. He woke just after dark, and from the front stoop he watched up and down Old Brownsville Road for her. He went around the side of the house and stood before the trellis. The garden spider had moved—gone—from its position in the center of the web. A moment, he thought about passing under the arch. Then he backed away from it and realized that his greatest fear was not the sight of the spider in its web, but the sight of it gone, the knowledge that it could be anywhere. And he thought about Casandra. Why didn't she wake him? What kind of woman is beaten and never makes a sound?

His mother came home late, long after he had fallen into an uneasy sleep.

Within a year, early the next summer, Casandra found a steady job checking groceries for a new quick-stop store, the Maverick. She and Eolo left their tiny tar-papered house and moved to a new apartment complex just off Old Brownsville Road. And part of Casandra's prophecy came to pass. Nothing after the moment he remembered his bruised mother walking down Old Brownsville Road remained the same. Never again did he taste the sweetness of honey, the bitter-clean of lemon, the drowsiness in a dose of aniseed tea, or feel the coolness of the egg in the same way. Never after that day did Eolo sleep with the scent of garlic or with the knowledge that Casandra kept vigil outside his window. He never again dreamed of the scorpion on the screen in his window or the spider in the garden trellis, or heard the once mysterious knocking at the front door in the vestiges of sleep.

Eventually, Eolo left Corpus Christi, and he did so with some urgency: when he left, he was a grown man, sure that his mother was insane most of his early life, and that it was only a matter of time and chance before he would have surrendered to her lunacy. Years after living with Casandra as a boy, he dreaded that her "point of breaking" had indeed occurred. He watched her carefully; he looked for signs of her old ways; he lay awake many nights in their new apartment waiting for her to come into his room and kneel by his bed. But she did not come, and with time he began to realize she had given up her old ways, and he slept like a dead man, refreshed each morning, pleased that she had become—not insane, by his reasoning—but so pleasantly ordinary.

Years after he had watched her tired, battered figure walking along Old Brownsville Road, he became more and more sure that she was completely—though mysteriously—cured. She led a quiet, uneventful, respectable life, and she retired from the Maverick store chain with an adequate pension and social security. At times he wondered if she would madly cling to him—her only son—as he had heard is the habit of the obsessed or insane. But he became more certain of this curious reversal, her recovery, when he announced he intended to leave for Cleveland, Ohio, to live with a cousin who had gotten him a job at the Regional Transit Authority there.

"I've heard it's a nice place," she said in a lucid, pleasant voice. "Very different from Corpus in some ways. Sounds like a decent job. Write when you get settled."

Eolo was not surprised when he came into a little money when Casandra died. In her last years, Casandra was a practical and frugal woman. He used the small inheritance to put himself through business school at Cleveland State, found a job with an investment firm, and married a woman of Welsh descent from Akron.

He was not intensely interested in finance, but he was well liked by the others in his office. He could often be seen downtown crossing Public Square. He wore fine gray suits, maroon ties against crisp white collars, and a long gold chain that extended from his vest pocket to his trousers. People who knew him in Cleveland admired his smile, not a protective smile, not the smile that hides the darkest secrets, or a chaos of mind and spirit, or the smile of those who are beautifully or obdurately insane, but a plain, everyday smile, a clear and pleasant smile, something akin to a harmless habit one acquires when one feels all is as it should be, or must be.

Still, Eolo lived years with a small dread that half of Casandra's prophecy would somehow become his own: that he too would become suddenly insane, would somehow find himself dreaming of the spider and the scorpion, and in deep and strange desire of the woman and her egg, her honey and anointing oil, her garlic—and her silent prattling lips in gloomy desperate prayer. But he led the most ordinary life, and like the memory of the tiny tar-papered house in Corpus

Christi, these bits of rubbish he eventually swept from the
smallest corners of his heart.

La Villa, La Villa Miseria

Gloria Milagras Durant sits on the sagging plank stoop of her father's house and sees into the South Texas gloaming. Across Old Brownsville Road, three dark-skinned men sit with their legs crossed in the grass behind the green clapboard shanty of S. Vásquez. Gloria sees their cigarette packs nearby on the rusted, upturned bottom of a wheelbarrow. The men smoke and laugh. One man has no shirt. He removes his hat and sets it in the dust beside him. He moves his head side to side and pauses when the sweep of his vision finds Gloria. But she sees no reason to shrink from his glance. She feels she knows him from his actions: how he has removed his hat, how his looking around himself, past the other two men sitting at the wheelbarrow, implies his silent astonishment at the dusk itself—the cooling atmosphere—his wonder that the coming of darkness can give something back, the cooler air which now creeps along the hot sideboards and clapboards of the shanties, broken cement walks, and plaster of Villarreal's Lounge, an ancient building which Gloria knows has become an oven stone under the white sun. Gloria does not know the man who has removed his hat, but she is certain he has come from the melon fields or cotton fields. His body is dark and strange like the waning light over the low tops of the shanties, dark on dark.

Gloria imagines in the full darkness the stories of her ancestors, as she has come to know them from Mariano, her father. A small laugh escapes her lips, *You see?* She laughs again, and she imagines Mariano's stories rising like a great impossible tree with many spiraling branches beside the baked and broken asphalt of Old Brownsville Road, an impossible tree because it does not live among the squat palm, diminutive pine, and mesquite trees of Corpus Christi. But Mariano's tree is shining and tall, and its branches spread in all directions, like Mariano's stories. *You see?* she sighs, and she cannot name his tree. It is simply Mariano's tree, and there are so many names in its branches! But she knows the stories in the impossible branches reaching over Old Brownsville Road, and over the three *emigrantes* sitting near the wheelbarrow.

Mariano Arambula Durant stands at the screen door behind Gloria. Mariano pushes the door open and she hears the spring whine where it is nailed to the door's frame. The door knocks shut and Mariano sits beside her. She feels his weight in the old wood of the porch, feels wood of the old stoop bow. She knows, seeing the small amber-faced man with his dust-colored hair, his soiled white T-shirt and cotton pants, she knows he will add to the impossible tales in his tree. "Cotez Gom, your great ancestor, was a famous artisan, a maker of the finest swords and armor. He lived in Madrid, *La Villa....* Oh, *chiquita,* he was so famous. A count, his patron, created the Gom coat of arms. Two magnificent swords were crossed in its middle, and behind them brilliant beams of light thrown to all sides.... Oh, *mi niña,* it was so gorgeous, and blessed by a priest! And the inscription—"

Across the road, the man who has removed his hat stands, and Gloria turns her head to watch him. One of the other men points to the hat on the ground. The man stoops, picks it up, and puts it on his head. The other men stand, and all three walk to the corner and Villarreal's Lounge. *Chiquita,* she thinks.... She is not such a little girl. Didn't Mariano know that?

"Don't you want to know the inscription?"

"Yes, Papa."

"*Armes Gom Sau Durant*. It means *The Weapons of Gom are Durable*. You see? You see, *chiquita*? The name *Durant*. This is you! *The Weapons of Gom are Durable*."

Gloria looks hard at Mariano, brings her knees to her chest, and holds them together with her arms. Mariano's tree begins to vanish from her mind. Through the new darkness, she hears the guitars at Villarreal's. They are muffled, tinny sounds through thick plastered walls, cracked wooden shutters, and iron bars over the windows.

"So what are you telling me, Papa? Swords and armor and Old Madrid. I am some kind of Spanish Joan of Arc?"

"No...but you see? Durant—durable. That's my name. That's your name. You see?"

"Yes, Papa."

"Good," Mariano sighs, "and good night."

Gloria waits until she hears Mariano snoring through the screen behind her, then she walks to Villarreal's. An easy chair with the batting coming out in clouds sits under three narrow windows, and beside it a small doghouse made of an overturned orange crate. The window shutters are dark and warped, and set behind rusted iron bars. Gloria notices only the tiniest creases of dim orange light in the cracks of the old shutters. The music is there behind the bars and shutters, but she can hear no more, no voices, no sounds of dancing or laughter. She sees only the light in the creases and hears the intimate sounds of the guitars. She walks back in the direction of her house. She never thinks of her house as a shanty, because it has three rooms. She passes her house and the shanty of S. Vásquez and those of several others who, unlike Vásquez, are *emigrantes*, and who she rarely sees. A light burns in one shanty. A box fan props the front door open. She pauses to listen to its blades turning in the damp air. Mariano's words return to her, *This is you. You see?* And she laughs a little, then she stops her little laugh...the dark-headed men... Mariano calls them little *blackheads*...

She passes an abandoned sheet-metal bending shop. The front portion of the roof is torn open, as if someone has taken a huge can opener to it. "You see?" she whispers, and she recalls the day her mother, Rosita, had passed as close to the shop as she did now, how the explosion killed her; she recalls two sobbing widows of the men working in the shop, their knees in the stones around the shop—and Mariano standing over them, looking into the sun until Gloria covered his eyes with her hands and tugged at him to come with her. Later, Mariano stood many hours near the stoop outside their house where Rosita's body lay; he stood silent and bareheaded in the blazing sun. He nearly died from the heat.

She recalls the strained and indecipherable outline of her mother's face—Rosita's face—the dark and placid face of Rosita Maria Durant. She stubs her toe on a crack in the walk and curses under her breath.

Earlier in the day the fire ants bit her between her toes, and now she feels the burden of walking. She senses the heat of the cement in the soles of her bare feet.... So soon after the sun sets the cement gives the heat of the day back to her. She is amazed and distressed by the ants and her feet and the hot cement. She is amazed at her existence. She thinks of her dead mother's feet, her cracked and broken toenails, the arthritis that reproportioned and disfigured her ankles into gnarled roots. But Rosita's hair was short, black, and luminous. *Durable?* she thinks, then she laughs her little laugh, *You see?*

Despite the pain in Gloria's feet, her little laugh seems to urge her on. She stops at the Hi-Ho, and goes through the service door to the kitchen. She looks at the slate menu hanging on the wall below the clock in the dining room—*Especiales: Lenguas y Tripas*. She cannot abide either, especially since Mariano likes her to cook them so often. She takes a tortilla from Mary's black, greased skillet, rolls it, and begins to eat it quickly, breathing hard through her nose as she chews. Mary comes into the kitchen, walks to the counter near her, shoves a stack of soiled plates aside with her rump, and leans there.

"You coming to work tonight, Gloria?—or you just some kind of lazy *puta?*"

Gloria tucks the last bit of tortilla into her mouth and sucks her fingertips loudly, one by one. Mary takes a ball of dough from her floured board and slaps it onto the counter.

"*¡Váyase!*" she says.

Gloria cooks Mariano's *lengua* in a pot on an old black stove in the back of the house. The propane is low, so she stoops to light the burner several times. She holds a match under the pot until she hears the flame pop. Mariano sits behind her at a small table. He has been painting, somewhere. He rubs his fingers over spots of white paint on his wrinkled brown hands. He catches a spot of paint with a fingernail and chisels it from his skin.

"You see, *chiquita,*" he says, "my great ancestor was the first Durant. He lived in La Villa. He fought the Moors in the south. Then he sailed to a tiny Dutch island in the Mediterranean where he met his wife. Then, like many famous Spaniards, he sailed to Cuba, where he grew tobacco and built *una hacienda grande*, and had many slaves...and he was good to his slaves, you see? Generations later, his descendant moved the family to Puerto Rico when the war with Cuba started. His descendant was a rich and respected man—and *chiquita*, he became a United States citizen when the island was made a territory—you see? This is you! A United States citizen!"

Gloria sets the table. She and Mariano eat. Later, she sponges Mariano's paint spots with turpentine. She soaks his clothes and lays out a fresh shirt and pair of trousers. When she finishes her chores, she rests on the old plank stoop. The three men return to the overturned wheelbarrow, where they set three brown bottles of beer. They sit and smoke and talk. Their faces are dirty and their eyes are slits under the harsh sun. Watching them, she feels lazy, supine, and dreamy. She sees their backs bending gradually upward from their buttocks to their shoulders, their heads hung low, the curve of their jaws as they talk and tip the brown bottles to their lips. She rises, crosses the street and stands near them. They pay no attention to her; then one man rises.

"*Chiquita*, you need a hat. You want my hat?"

The man grins, and she sees his teeth etched brown on all edges by tobacco. She imagines her great ancestor's tobacco plantation, the slaves, their backs bent under the sun among the broad, curved tobacco leaves. The man waves his hat at her. The other men laugh, and she returns to the stoop, where she meets Mariano and they walk together to the Church of the Holy Family.

On the way to the church, Mariano begins another story.

"My father met his wife in Eagle Pass, the shallowest part of the Rio Grande, across from Piedras Negras in Mexico. There was a great love affair. For one year he wrote letters to Luisa—and he never set eyes on her. But he wrote beautiful and respectful letters, and the families arranged for them to meet, and for two more years he courted her in the old way. You see?"

Gloria thinks of her mother, her small black-headed mother, whose tongue ran rapid fire, who walked among *los emigrantes* with so much ease. A question forms in her mind, but she knows the answer, or she can save it for later. The question vanishes when she looks at Mariano's face and sees it smiling, splayed with wrinkles.

The Church of the Holy Family is part of an old mission. Its exterior is patched, and through the new paint and plaster Gloria sees the cracks running from the corners of the doorposts and window frames, and fanning over its frontispiece. Here, too, she sees the branches of Mariano's tree, and as she waits for him to finish confession, she studies the fourteen

Stations of the Cross hanging along the wall. She focuses only on the orientation of the cross, how it moves and pitches left and right in each successive frame. At last, she sees the cross straight up. Then she imagines the fourteen stations laid on top of each other so that the images of the cross in all its various orientations become a tree of beams and crossbeams, and it seems unreal to her. *Váyase*, she says under her breath.

Inside the confessional, Gloria hears Father Lynch rustle his robes. He breathes and sighs.

"Go on," he says.

"Forgive me, Father, for I have sinned..."

"Go on."

"I took a tortilla from Mary's pan at the Hi-Ho's."

She hears his robes again, and the sound of his back leaning into the wall at the far side of the confessional.

"Go on."

"I wanted to take God's name in vain. I stubbed my toe and I wanted to say.... I mean I think I said it under my breath. I wanted to curse the fire ants for biting my feet."

"Go on."

His voice is more distant, and Gloria pauses a moment. She searches her mind for more—*what else*? She thinks of the three men outside her house and the music at Villarreal's. There must be more.

"I have been disrespectful to my father.... I mean I have disrespectful thoughts."

The priest pauses. She hears him lean forward in the booth. She hears him breathing. She imagines by his voice he is more interested.

"In what way have you disrespected him?"

"He tells me stories. The truth is he is a liar. Shouldn't he tell you himself if he is a liar? He should be confessing—did he?"

"My child!" the priest says, pauses, then adds, calmly, "What kinds of stories are these?"

"About his family, his ancestors. He makes them up. He lies and lies...swords and armor, counts and rich land barons, coats of arms, fighting the Moors, all about *La Villa* in Spain. It's like some fabulous tree. He lies and lies—you see?"

"You must try to believe him. He is your father. Go on. Anything else?"

Gloria thinks, and the more she thinks, the more she is confused. Why must there always be more? Then she puts her fingers to her lips and she thinks harder. She pinches her lips together with the tips of her fingers and a sigh of delight escapes her mouth.

"Yes, Father, I asked him if he thought I was some kind of Joan of Arc."

Gloria is pleased with herself. Five *Our Fathers* and one *Hail Mary*. The priest had let her off easy. And her remark about Joan of Arc ended the confession her way, and left him speechless. She walks home briskly with Mariano at her side, thinking of before Mass and her confession with Father Lynch. She is even more pleased. She should have made him hear more. Was there more? Villarreal's? The three men in back of Vásquez's? She let the priest go too soon. And who ever heard of five *Our Fathers* and only one *Hail Mary? Mariano, you see? Won't the Blessed Virgin be upset?* She makes a little laugh.

Near dusk, Mariano and Gloria sit on the sagging plank stoop. Gloria turns her attention to the backs of the three men who come again in the gloaming to sit by the overturned wheelbarrow. With her eyes she measures the tiny distances between the shanties, with her nose the smell of dust, sweat, and garbage at the back of Hi-Ho's that dogs have dragged into the street. She sees the shanty of S. Vásquez across Old Brownsville Road, and the fan turning inside the front door, and the remnants of the explosion at the sheet-metal shop that killed her mother. She feels the gloaming and the waning heat, now tepid in the air, now nearly nothing to the senses, a memory of the day, now lifeless. Here, she hopes for a miracle, a push of wind, this way or that, a sudden nudge of air against her skin, a change, but there is nothing. And in this moment of perfect stillness wrapped over her like a thick dirty blanket, she wants to strip it off and blow back the gloaming and the stillness with words.

"Oh my, *chiquita*," Mariano says. "My great uncle's house in La Villa was so white, with high, clean walls, and a perfect arch leading to the patio in front, a patio tiled with smooth squares of pink marble, and there was a pure white statute of the Virgin and a fountain, and all around the patio were azaleas with deep-green glossy leaves and flaming red flowers." Gloria bites her fingernails. She is half-turned to Mariano, and he becomes animated as he speaks of his great uncle's house in La Villa. He puts his arms out and uses the flat of his palms to place the objects of his uncle's great house in the air. He has never spoken so passionately of La Villa, and Gloria becomes slightly intoxicated with his words. "And the air was clear and cool and carried the light of brilliant days. The light all the days was lavender, and the sun in the skies over La Villa cool and orange and red over my great uncle's house— ¡mira! This is you! In a grand hacienda with lawns so green and wide on all sides..."

Mariano moves his arms in wide circles and sharply at many angles, painting with each motion the garden and house in La Villa. The more his arms wave and wander in the air, the more the wood in the plank wearies under his weight until it breaks in two and Mariano and Gloria drop to the ground.... Mariano holds his hands on top of his head. Gloria laughs her little laugh, "You see?" And she wants the little laugh back, but it is too late. "This is not La Villa, Papa," she whispers. "You see?"

She watches Mariano's shoulders sink and his hands come down from his head and rest at his sides. He turns from her and looks straight into the gloaming. A moment, Gloria feels, he might also wish to blow the still air away, but there is no change in him. He is silent, a silence she knows will last.

She rises and stands near the broken plank stoop until the three men around the wheelbarrow also rise and walk to Villarreal's. She follows them at a distance. She stops at the back of the building until the three men round the corner to the front. She hears the door swing open and guitar music spill into the air. Then she hears the door shut, but she hears the music continue in the wall behind her. The music sounds strange and intimate. It seems trapped in the plaster itself. The still air has trapped her, and now the music. She backs into the wall and the music increases. She leans her back to the wall and presses her arms to it. She feels the heat of the oven stone give back the heat of the long day, give back the heat of the cement walks and shanties and boiled *lenguas y tripas*, the bent and browned backs of the workers in the fields. She feels all of it, all that has been saved for later, saved for the daylong sun's final insult to *la villa miseria*, how it gives back just one thing.... Then, there before her, Mariano's tree rises, first a thick trunk and one great cross timber, and from these gigantic limbs many branches twist up and out in unending helical spires. *To where?* she asks, and she feels the oven stone and the heat burning more intensely through her back to her heart. The heat courses through her, and the music in Villarreal's, and the need to take all that the oven stone will give, and to burn, burn Mariano's tree. She makes her little laugh. *You see?* There will be plenty of stories, plenty from now on, plenty to tell the priest.

Soledad

*Yet ev'n these bones from insult
to protect,
Some frail memorial still
erected nigh,
With uncouth rhymes and
shapeless sculpture deck'd
Implores the passing tribute of
a sigh.*

—Thomas Gray, "Elegy Written in
a Country Church-Yard"

*I pulled myself together, of course.
What did one man's lie matter in
the history of generations?*

—Albert Camus, *The Fall*

I am the youngest of Blanche Sylvia Hammonds's three children, an odd position in the chronologies of pregnancy and birth, birth and pregnancy for Blanche Sylvia, all neatly two years apart. And because I am her last child, I never had the occasion to observe her pregnancies and the births of my older siblings, and, of course, how could I recall my own? So I have this view of our family as newly arrived, as put here on stage, all our cast winning their parts over others, and here, in our first performance in Corpus Christi, we moved through our cues, and we spoke terse, clear lines, but not Blanche Sylvia. I named Mother Blanche Sylvia because her first and middle names had a certain vague beauty, and as I grew older, I also sensed a strange ambivalence in the two names taken together: one washed of color, the other lush, leafy, and green. And like the name I gave her, Blanche Sylvia defied definition. She won me with ways I did not understand and still do not. But let me move on to things of which I am certain...

We Hammonds have never been a family of words. What words we have lend themselves to certainty and create a kind of transportable mythology that surrounds us. We carry it with us, and we generally keep it to ourselves. We do not speak of it, yet we know our mythology with as much certainty as the orthography of our names. We have no nicknames, although Father sometimes calls us You, collectively or individually, when he is angry. Otherwise, only our proper names sound as they are called round and round in the same ways day after day, and we all believed the mythology of our names, even as it regarded Blanche Sylvia.

Devlin was Blanche Sylvia's oldest, and when I think of him, I believe I came to know him through the myth of the Lacerated Fingers. One day, Mary, Blanche Sylvia's second child, and I were playing with an enormous floor fan in our aunt's living room in Amarillo. The fan was made of a heavy hardwood and stained darkly. Long, thin ribbons of metal ran down the front and back of the fan to protect one's fingers from the large blades. Mary and I knelt behind the fan and pressed our faces to the ribbons and began to say silly things into the turning blades. We marveled at how our voices were transformed, and made a stiff mechanical vibrato by the chopping blades. Of course, my fingers found their way through the ribbons of metal: I parted the ribbons, pushed my fingers close to the blades and—*thwang!*—I began to cry without looking at three long gashes running diagonally across my knuckles. Mary sat stunned. Devlin rushed into the room, fell to his knees, and pressed my fingers gently between his hands.

"Shut up," he whispered nervously, looking side to side for our parents and aunt. "Come on, shut up."

Father came in, snatched my hand from Devlin's, examined it briefly, and shut off the fan. He held my hand in front of Mary and Devlin and waved it like a dead leaf at them. By that time, I was wailing as loud as my lungs would allow, not so much from pain, but from Father's presence, and how he made my mangled hand a public matter. My eyes fogged over and I closed them tightly to try to keep the tears from running out of them.

"How did this happen?" Father growled.

For Father, a university teacher of physics, there was always an answer, and knowing this only exacerbated my anguish. Father let go of my hand, and I screamed and began to slap my arms at my sides. Then Father, Mary, and Devlin turned to me with expressions of absolute amazement on their faces. At once, I sensed that the matter of my bawling was more urgent than my bleeding fingers. They stared at me with their jaws hanging in disbelief that so much noise could come from anyone in our secure, silent family. I caught my breath, opened my eyes wide and stared back at them; then, seeing how utterly shocked they seemed, began bawling all over again. And I pointed at Devlin with my good hand.

"You," Father said to Devlin.

Father abruptly rose and left the room to find Blanche Sylvia, who was outside in my aunt's garden.

We have never been a family of words, so guilt was always a sure substitute for real pain. Father never hit Devlin, and in those early days this amazed us, but Father's single-syllable reproaches, followed by stone silence, and the glares the accused received from behind his thick, black, horn-rimmed glasses were nothing less than a death sentence—or at least a long, long stint in solitary.

Blanche Sylvia came into the room and she said a few soft words to me. She led me to the sink in the kitchen to wash my wounds. Mary followed us and Devlin stayed behind, alone in the living room near the dangerous fan, still on his knees.... As I said, I was never privy, in even the most circuitous way, to the creation myths of my family, such as the bringing home of a new baby sister or brother (and certainly the idea of conception had not dawned on me), so the glimpse I had of Devlin as Blanche Sylvia hustled me away to the kitchen, Devlin with his hands on his knees, his head bent down, his bearing the wrong I had done him, was my first sense of the drama of life: the flesh made parable. Here was my brother, the scapegoat. He had saved me. He bore Father's single-syllable wrath. And now I realized our individual myths had two parts: the part that made us each unique, and the part that made us each alone.

A new piece of our transportable family mythology followed shortly after the Lacerated Fingers: the myth of Miraculous Change. Blanche Sylvia stood at our aunt's sink scrubbing my knuckles under the flowing faucet. She lathered her hands, then my knuckles. She rinsed my knuckles. She did not ask what had happened or who did it. She scrubbed harder and I winced with pain. I saw Mary. She wanted to speak, and I was relieved to see her wish to speak because it intrigued me and turned my attention from the soaping and stinging of my wounds. She said to Blanche Sylvia, "Will you make tortillas tonight?—and okra? I'll help you in the garden."

Suddenly, the world changed, a sudden, marvelous change. Blanche rinsed my traumatized knuckles once more and dried them with a towel. She smiled, and I remember her smile made her smooth-skinned face grow oddly darker. Her skin was usually dark, but set in the sharp frame of her short glossy, black hair, it seemed less dark. But when she smiled her face became suddenly, radiantly dark.

"Yes," Blanche Sylvia said, and she took my wounded hand and Mary's and led us to our aunt's garden where she had been weeding before the catastrophe with the floor fan. There, in the okra poking from their stems like tiny rockets, I knelt beside Blanche Sylvia. I noticed Mary standing behind us. Despite her promise to help Blanche Sylvia, she stood and

watched us pick okra. Mary folded her arms and seemed satisfied: she had averted Blanche Sylvia's distress over my
wound, and at the same time contracted for Blanche Sylvia's
mighty tortillas and sublime okra. Yet she stood alone, apart
from us, and I believed in that moment only Mary, alone,
could have accomplished this great change.

In contrast to Blanche Sylvia's vaguely dark complexion
framed in her black hair, Father's hair was red, red as skin
scalded, and it laid over his forehead in a great wave that rose
from a deep part on the left side of his head. He wore black
slip-on shoes, dark wrinkled slacks, and thick, horn-rimmed
glasses. But all Father's features, especially his great red
crest of hair, were made into drama the first time I saw him
raise his hand and bat Devlin's fingers away from his red
crest. Who could blame Devlin? His curiosity about Father's
hair got the better of him, and thus poor Devlin was there at
the inception of the myth of the Forbidden Red Crest.

It was not the curious and startling crest of hair alone
that made Father larger than life, but the place where we
lived. In Corpus Christi, the coarse and struggling follicles of
plant and scrub surrounded us: the grasses, prickly pear cacti,
short, squat palms with their dry, shaggy manes sticking out
against the coolish blue of the sky; the bowed, brown, and glis-
tening backs of the pickers in the cotton fields. All of this grew
in the interstices between the earth and cement, asphalt,
gravel, and crushed fossils and shells that lay over the berms
and the sides of walks... and all this under the clear and present sun. Father's blazing hair and the yellow eye of the sun
presided over Corpus, and tempted one to touch things so brilliant. And when Father batted Devlin's hand from his red
crest, I suddenly realized that the surprising stings of the
prickly pear or the serrated fronds of the palms were to warn
people away, to say they wanted to be left alone. Father was
alone in his way, too.

Father taught physics at Corpus Christi State University,
and considering I had created his role in our family with such

precision, he was supremely inaccessible. And one June, when he announced we would be moving a great distance to Athens, Ohio later that summer, I became sure he would remain that way. He told us he had been offered a teaching position. As he made the announcement, he pricked his glasses from his nose and licked each lens with a swipe of his tongue. Then he drew a handkerchief from his back pocket and wiped the lenses.

"Everyone see?" he said.

But I had questions, and most of them I could not even phrase, but then we were not a family to raise many questions, and these unarticulated matters collected and piled around Father, until I could not help but feel they buried him from sight.

We were not a family of words, but despite this I grew accustomed to the certainty of our unspoken roles. Devlin had saved me, and he continued to save me whenever I pointed an accusatory finger—what stamina of spirit! Mary, with the most innocent suggestions to Blanche Sylvia—and as her powers grew, to Father—could bring about the most gracious and sweeping changes. Her soft, tiny words blew through our lives like stiff and sudden bursts of cool wind from the Gulf. But Blanche Sylvia remained a puzzle: when I expected her to be mending arguments, she allowed them, and mended clothes instead. When I expected her to begin a fray, she took to trimming the loose threads of our shirts. When I expected her to bear one of my tantrums, she slipped away from me to the kitchen to boil a pot of beans or to roll and press out her mighty tortilla dough for the evening meal. But I watched her. When I was not in school, I followed her throughout the house. I trailed her night and day. I questioned Devlin and Mary about her in various situations:

She put a dent in Father's car.

"What did she do?"

"She told him the car dents too easily!"

She caught Devlin with Father's cigarettes.

"What did she do?"

"She smoked them herself!"

I looked for some archetypal pattern to assign a certain meaning to Blanche Sylvia's life, to somehow position her in our clan, but I could not. In each situation, she behaved unexpectedly, without reason, and this became the source of lengthy discussions among her children. We would gather in the yard behind Father's shed, and whisper, "Father said... and she did what?"

"Who would have thought!"

So I was not surprised when one Saturday afternoon before we moved north, and while Father was away at a seminar in San Antonio, Blanche Sylvia hustled us into the car, and drove, drove, and drove for hours. I slept much of the way, waking from time to time to see if I could get my bearings. But I couldn't. And as we traveled farther, I woke more frequently, and found myself noting the precise names of towns we passed: Alice, Rosita, Catarina.... They were such pretty, concise, and certain names, which made me feel a little secure that far out in West Texas. The names differentiated themselves nicely, but the landscape did not. It was flat and desolate, sparsely populated by scrub plants and tiny, low, white, wood frame houses, and road signs all the same shape, all indicating this or that—and WEST, always WEST. I scrunched down in my seat and began to kick at Devlin's leg, which should have caused a minor squabble, but Devlin, always in character, soon quelled the dispute by moving to the window seat and putting Mary in the middle between us. He knew I'd never kick her. And it was then I noticed how odd it was that Blanche Sylvia had not hustled any of us into the front seat to sit with her. She drove alone, nudging the wheel a little left, a little right. She held her head high and still. I dozed, and when I woke I found Blanche Sylvia precisely in the same posture behind the wheel, and noticed how the wind through the window vent took a few strands of her limp black hair and whipped them against the crease between her ear and neck.

After four hours, I was wide awake and began to wonder why no one asked the Inevitable Question. At last, Devlin spoke:

"Where are we going? How much longer?"

"We're here," Blanche Sylvia said, and she moved the wheel left and pulled into a filling station. I, of course, noticed the sign: *Estación de Servicio*. Blanche Sylvia put gas in the car while I wondered why she had driven four hours just to fill the gas tank. As she was handing cash to a thin man standing in the doorway to the office, I saw Devlin bump Mary's arm.

"Listen," he said to Mary. "Do you hear her talking?"

The thin man raised his arm and pointed south to a bluff dotted with scrub pine. Blanche Sylvia chattered in bursts of Spanish. The thin man chattered back to her in Spanish after each of her bursts. He lowered his arm when he responded to her, then raised it to point again in the same direction. I watched Devlin with his mouth hanging down as he listened to Blanche Sylvia's foreign tongue.

"Who would have thought!" he said.

The wide afternoon sky, which had whitened and washed the color from the land, now grew dim, and the clouds lay in orange and red streaks across it. The sun painted the land pink and purple, and the shadows over the scrub and desert grew narrow and sharp, like those cast by dozens of gnomon. Blanche Sylvia seated herself behind the wheel and drove south toward a shallow notch in the bluff the man had pointed to. I noticed a sign for the town of Eagle Pass and another for Piedras Negras, what I now know to be *Black Rocks*, in Mexico. She pulled the car to the side of the narrow road near the right shoulder of the shallow notch and got out. She motioned us out of the car and we followed her to the Rio Grande. We waded into the thin sheets of brown water at the river's edge. From there, in the distance, I saw the pile of black rocks for the first time. Blanche Sylvia sat in the water with her legs up. She cupped her hands, dipped them into the water, raised them, and allowed the water to run through her fingers, over her cheeks, and down her neck. We did not speak while we were in the river. Blanche Sylvia seemed satisfied, and her three children were satisfied, and there were no more discussions among us of her imponderable behavior, including our long drive west in Father's absence. Only Devlin dared to speak as the light left the sky and we left the river.

"Where are your mother and father?" he asked Blanche Sylvia.

I did not see her gesture as she responded, but her voice carried in the new dark air.

"There," she said, "in the rocks."

The next week we packed and moved far north to Athens.

I am certain Blanche Sylvia never told Father about our trip to Piedras Negras, and as certain Devlin and Mary hadn't either. Such gossip is not our way.

Father bought several acres on a wooded hill south of Athens, off County Road 19. Father took up his teaching duties, and we lived comfortably on the wooded hill, and in the changing seasons I forgot the clear white light of Texas and the land washed of color by the sun.

We carried our personal myths with us—they had not suffered for the trip. Devlin reassumed his role as martyr, Mary as miracle worker, Father as forbidden, and Blanche Sylvia…chimera? I wondered as I grew older if the idea of her as a foolish or impossible fantasy was a mythic role at all. Would she ever conform to some reasonable way of my seeing her?

Words were always a premium among us, but we continued to confess our amazement at Blanche Sylvia's behavior: she sent a washer repair man packing because he used the

word *hell* in a casual way; she did similarly with many repre-
sentatives of the service industry who visited our house on the
hill. I entered the middle school, and Mary and Devlin were
finishing high school. But as they grew older, Mary and
Devlin began to lose their words for Blanche Sylvia, and I was
alone in my quest to accurately ascribe an essence to her.
Their silence about Blanche Sylvia became complete when she
took off unexpectedly one morning, as Father told us, to visit
friends in Corpus Christi. But I did not give up. I waited for
her to return, and not having her to stalk around the house
after school or on weekends, I began to follow Mary and
Devlin. But they became angry and told me to go away.

During Blanche Sylvia's absence, Father started to take
shots from the whiskey bottle he kept in the cupboard for the
rare occasions we had company. Mary cooked. Devlin drove by
that time, so he shopped; and I, I did little or nothing, perhaps
because I could hardly bear the upheaval Blanche Sylvia's
absence had caused. I was shocked when Devlin blamed *me*
for breaking a plate as I carried it to the sink after dinner for
him to wash. In front of Father!

"You," Father said to me, opened the cupboard, and
reached for his bottle.

Of course, I had broken the plate, but this was not the
issue! And little Mary broke the pervasive silence in the house
and began to challenge Devlin and me on a number of issues:
the chores we assigned her, the way we called her "little." She
no longer made her stunning and graceful proposals to keep
the peace. She pursued her arguments tooth and nail. We
became unglued. We forgot our parts, lost our lines, bungled
our cues completely!

I could hardly contain myself when Blanche Sylvia
returned after a month's absence. But I do not believe I was
overjoyed because I was a spoiled son. When she returned,
Father stopped draining his whiskey supply, Devlin stopped
letting the blame for my actions fall on me, and, miraculously,
Mary stopped her bickering and regained her powers of steer-

ing us away from ourselves when we most needed it. Blanche
Sylvia was in her home in the great, cold north, and all was
right with the world, though I could not ultimately say why.
Her presence was still as indecipherable as I found her name:
Blanche, white, washed, vague and colorless, erased, and
Sylvia, Sylvanus, Sylvan, one who should be at home in the
woods—but was she? Father had moved her into the very
environment that should have suited her, so when she left our
piney hill a second time to visit Texas, she left me even more
confused. Why couldn't she just stay put? Father grew especially tired and thin, and dark rings formed around his eyes.
His red hair thinned and darkened. He became an anemic rac-
coon. Nights, he paced the kitchen. I could hear him rummaging in the cupboards for his whiskey, knocking bottles and
glasses about. That he was sullen and withdrawn were the
only vestiges of his former self I recognized. Just who were
these friends Blanche Sylvia visited? I had a right to know. I
had spent my whole life studying the woman.

When I could bear her absence no longer, I began my own
rummaging. Father taught a seminar Monday nights, and
while Blanche Sylvia was in Texas I searched the drawers in
her bedroom. I searched her closet. I did this three Mondays
straight. During my third search I found a Polaroid photograph that had partly fallen between the seams in the wood at
the bottom of one drawer. In the photograph were the black
rocks near Piedras Negras across the Rio Grande. Blanche
Sylvia was centered in the photograph at the base of the
rocks. She stood straight and small and smiling against the
tall dark shapes. Someone must have taken this photograph.
Her friends? Some friends they must be to draw her so regu-
larly from her family—from *me*!

When Blanche Sylvia returned from her third trip to
Texas, she stayed with us a solid six months, and during that
time she became unglued. She sat long hours staring out at
the pines around our house. Once she cut all the electric cords
in the house, which Devlin, fearing Father's single-syllable

wrath, dutifully repaired as best he could. She refused to step near anything even vaguely metallic. Nights, she paced the house half-clothed, and Father hustled her from our sight.

Father cut a path through the woods to a small clearing at the bottom of the hill near Fox Lake, hoping Blanche Sylvia would get outside more, but she would not leave the house. On one of her more lucid days, she told Father she wanted a piano, so Father bought her one, and in the hours just before dawn I heard her strike the keys at random and call out the names of colors: blue and pink and black and orange.... She grew hard and strange and never cried in even her most bizarre moods.

Father enrolled Blanche Sylvia in an outpatient program. He tried pills and therapy. She threw away the pills and refused to attend the sessions. Through my bedroom wall I heard the muffled sounds of Father's long monologues to her late at night.

"A little chemical imbalance," Father explained to us when he saw our expressions of disbelief and exhausted all other explanations.

The night before Blanche Sylvia apparently threw herself into Fox Lake at the bottom of the path Father cleared, I found the word SOLEDAD spray-painted in vibrant red on the kitchen wall over the stove.

Father never forgave me for only attending the viewing of Blanche Sylvia's body, but not the burial of her ashes in the small clearing at the bottom of the wooded path. For one thing, Blanche Sylvia once told me Father reserved the spot for all our ashes. I could not bear to see it before *my* time. I did not need to see her ashes put into the ground. And it was enough to see her body before they burned it, enough to see the bridge of her nose, and when I edged a little closer to the casket, the same tuft of back hair curled in the crease between her neck and ear that had whipped free in the air as she drove us years before to the shallow, muddy waters of the Rio Grande.

"You," Father said when he saw me sitting in the kitchen staring at the word Blanche Sylvia had painted over the stove.

I recall feeling that Father wanted to add a second word after his dolorous "You," but none came, and he tucked his chin to his chest and left me to ponder Blanche Sylvia's word on the wall: SOLEDAD. Of course, my penchant for few but certain words drove me to consult a Spanish-English dictionary that very night at the university library: *solitude*, it read, or *loneliness*... but which one? There, in the library, instead of being in deep mourning for my mother, I held the dictionary in my lap and became angry and suddenly aware of the perverseness of my anger. I could not mourn or deeply feel her death until I straightened out the language of her life. Even in death, she defied me; she would not be defined. Which was it? Had she needed solitude, or been, simply, clinically lonely? And what great matter could either have been to her? Years, I looked around at Devlin, Mary, and Father, and observed with clarity and accuracy their outward behaviors, and justified quite clearly to myself the causes of their own special prisons, their loneliness—but *solitude*? What was this? And had she meant *her* solitude? Or was there some general condition of existence I was missing? How—even in death—could she have left me in such a quandary, a single, foreign word written by a deceased hand? A word with so many meanings? *Soledad*. The only word I knew her by was as muddy as the Rio Grande—and I believed I hated her for it.

Mary and Devlin, of course, left home and went on to college. In my turn, I was the last to leave Father's house in the pines, and I carried Blanche Sylvia's *Soledad*, her last utterance and ambiguity with me. I carried it to college, where I graduated and found work as an accountant. How fitting, I thought: all my life I liked to keep the books straight. I carried Blanche Sylvia's word with me to my first and second mar-

riages, both brief and without children. I carried it in and out
of bachelorhood, until the very word itself began to condition
me for every part I played—student, professional, husband,
ex-husband, malcontent.... I found myself exhausted. I began
to doubt the circumstances of my very being—my beginnings.
How could I be the offspring of the Forbidden Red Crest and
an enigma? With what certainty could I be sure I was not
adopted, or a black-market baby?

I never returned to see Father in eight years. I lost track
of Mary and Devlin. I had no obligations. So I flew to Corpus
Christi and visited the Nueces County Courthouse. There, I
purchased a copy of my birth certificate, and found it in order.
And I found Blanche Sylvia's maiden name: BLANCHE
SYLVIA GONZALEZ. Yet, I was only slightly surprised. I long
suspected she carried an Hispanic surname, but how could I
believe Blanche Sylvia would have so suddenly and drastically
despaired over *her* family by *that* surname? I didn't trouble
that much over *my* family. Thus, stonewalled, I continued to
collect what else I could. I found a copy of Father's and
Blanche Sylvia's marriage license. I found the certificate to be
in order, though I was curious about the other names on both
documents, the nurse, the doctor, the witnesses who must
have seen the amazing marriage of Father and Blanche Sylvia
or who were present at my birth at 5:04 a.m. August 15, 1951.
But this curiosity soon subsided.

I asked the clerk to look for Blanche Sylvia's birth certificate. I wrote her name on a slip of paper, BLANCHE SYLVIA
GONZALEZ, and handed it to the clerk along with the date of
her birth, December 7, 1930, a personal fact I did manage to
squeeze from Blanche Sylvia after years of diligent inquiry.
The clerk went away, then came back and handed my slip of
paper to me. The clerk said she could not find it. Since I was
fairly certain Blanche Sylvia was born in Nueces County, I
reasoned she had either lied about her age or been born at
home. I suspected these things, but they were not very exciting to me. So I left the courthouse, somewhat disappointed,

but on my way to my rented car I spotted a sign for the city library, and saw what I believed to be a bit of its roof behind the courthouse. At the library, I found, quite by accident, a Texas genealogy section on the second floor, where a flat-chested woman with long auburn hair and freckles showed me to a drawer of microfiche. I searched the microfiche with a lazy curiosity. I searched all the births in Texas in 1930, and there among the listed births in Nueces County I found only one on December 7, 1930: BLANCHE SOLEDAD GONZALEZ.

Was it such a little thing?—first the erasure of her maiden name, then, somehow, of her middle name, her Christian name, a name handed down among Spanish-speaking peoples from her grandmother: SOLEDAD? But where were her people now? How did they vanish? Had they all, too, erased their names? If so, who had been behind the Polaroid camera at Piedras Negras?—Blanche Soledad herself, a delayed exposure? And what did this erasure of her last two names leave? BLANCHE? How vague and blank. How unfull and untelling.

Shortly after my visit to Texas, I visited Father with my little words—*Sylvia, Soledad*—and found him not surprised by my visit. He sat in the screened porch in front of the house in Athens and waved his hand limply at me as I walked up to the door. I went onto the porch and glanced through the windows to see if I could spot his empty whiskey bottles. I found none, and Father seemed lucid and clear-minded, resting in a wicker chair.

"You," he said.

"Yes, me," I replied and lowered myself into a chair near him. I watched his eyes. I watched for the faintest sign of weakness in them, and saw a momentary softening below the fearsome porch of his thinning, but still vibrant red crest. I was sure he was thinking about Blanche Sylvia, and I struck while I had the chance.

"Blanche Sylvia's middle name was Soledad, wasn't it?"

"What?" he said, and he paused. I watched his jaw tense, and he continued. "It is a little matter—a word. Especially in those days. She was never much with words. I gave her that name. In fact, I named all of you."

He rose, turned, and went through the door to the house, pausing with it open a crack. Then he let the door slip from his fingers and knock gently against the frame. I expected he wanted me to follow him...

When I left Father, I walked the gravel drive a short distance to the wooded path Father had cut. There, I found a good stick for my hike to the grave site. I remember the pines, their trunks running straight and thick around me. The sky was overcast, but plenty of light fell through the trees. The wind died, and at a slight bend in the path I saw red-brown checkerings through a stand of poplar saplings in a patch of pale-green fern. I believed it to be a fox or perhaps a wild dog, but the instant I pushed my stick to the ground and came forward, the instant I recognized the slim form of a new deer, a doe whose spots had turned into vague, linear patches of silver in her coat, she leapt over the ferns and through the trees, her white tail high and arrow-like. I was amazed at her color as she streaked through the dark, vertical lines of the pines until I lost her. I stood amazed that she did not make a single sound against the trees or brush in her escape.... I caught my breath and thought... *Blanche Sylvia?*

But I never completed my walk to the grave site and what I knew would be a greening brass nameplate engraved, BLANCHE SYLVIA HAMMONDS. Perhaps I could not go because I am not a man of many words, and men of few words are good at keeping secrets, but not at uncovering them. And I have no more room for secrets. Times, I believe I have only room for *Soledad*, and I have carried it with me all these years.... Perhaps it is better than carrying ashes or memories, better than lugging around the certainties of lineage that splay through other lives like the hungry hard branches of a spreading tree. Perhaps it is far better to carry just one word when one drives great distances into the desert, easier to sound just one word in blues and reds and blacks that far from the crowded world, from the cities of competing sounds. Perhaps it is more practical to hear oneself utter a single word, easier for the vast desert skies to hear it, the rocks to send it back, the solitary mind to contemplate the intonation and stress of each isolated vowel and consonant. *Soledad...* perhaps such a single word is more suited to a living soul—or a dead one—and as easily suited to the single spark from my campfire that spirals up and dies in the night sky near Piedras Negras, where I often dream of my ancestors, see them in the tongue of flame, in the faces among the black rocks, and call their names in the impossible song of my impossible race.

New Moon

Zost, my neighbor, conducts his patio party from a yellow-webbed aluminum lawn chair. A wire runs down from behind his ear to the Walkman in his lap. I can hear the tinny beat of what he's picking up in his earplug.

The sky is blue and the clouds are riding high. They move fast. It's breezy, but hot.

I shift a little right in my chair, feel skin on my chest wrinkle around the scar of the operation, a familiar tug. I shift back, listen to Zost, who tells me how he *plumb forgets* to invite the García woman to these affairs. Then he's back with *Madonna* and the top forty.

Now he says he's glad he's a pharmacist; pharmacists do well in Houston, no matter what the price of crude oil.

Mrs. Zost lays out liver pâté, pumpernickel, and sweet pickles on a silver dish. She says she never brings the platter out except for special occasions—she giggles—*a wedding present, you know what I mean?*

Chan and his wife are sitting with me at a round redwood deck table. A yellow shade umbrella hovers over it, cocked to one side. The Chans are both chubby. He's a high school football coach. Chan says what he said at the party last weekend—*it's really not so difficult to imagine...many Chinese have never seen, nor would they care to see, Mainland China.*

The Chans are drinking beer from *Star Wars* glasses. Zost got them at Burger King. Chan holds his glass up to the sun. "A real nice set," he says to Zost, who can't hear him over the Walkman.

Hansen is my other neighbor, a thin, pale-skinned man, an engineer of some specific variety for an oil firm. Hansen stands by Zost's back door, running his eyes up and down the Zosts' new cedar siding. Hansen never sits at these affairs. He reconnoiters, like he's blueprinting things in his head.

Hansen's wife wears a printed sun dress; she goes over to Mrs. Chan, dragging a lawn chair with her. Mrs. Hansen spreads the chair out and sits with Chan's wife. She turns a tumbler of Rob Roy in her hands. Zost's specialty drink.

"I don't think I've ever seen the García woman," Mr. Hansen says, kneeling by the air conditioner, peering into the metal ventilation slots.

"Poor dear. She works such long hours," Mrs. Hansen says. "I think she's a widow."

Mr. Hansen calls over from Zost's back door. He's pouring a beer. "I don't exactly keep banker's hours," he says.

"I didn't mean it that way, Hon," Mrs. Hansen says. "All I mean," she says wearily, "is that the García woman was out mowing her lawn in a long white evening dress one morning this week."

"Really..." Chan says.

"...and she was mowing like 6:30 a.m."

"It's odd..." Mrs. Zost says. She comes around the deck table and puts the dish of liver pâté squarely in front of me. "Try this. I put crushed pecans in it this time."

"It's not so odd," Zost pulls the Walkman wire from his ear. "I think the homeowners' association sent the García woman a letter about the upkeep of her lawn."

Mrs. Hansen tips the Rob Roy to her lips and sets the tumbler back on the deck table. "Well, let's give her *some* credit," Mrs. Hansen says. "She now knows the storm sewers are not the place to dump her grass clippings."

There is scattered laughter around me. Mrs. Chan is wagging her head. "That's a good one," she says. She turns to her husband. "Hon, you should go over to García's and show that woman how to use her power mower—poor dear!—it's self-propelled, and she's pushing it around by brute force!"

"Tell her yourself," Chan says to his wife, and he gets up to join Hansen, who is asking Zost how far he's sunk his footers for the new fence he's putting in. Hansen and Zost walk to the back of Zost's yard to examine the new fence.

"...and how she keeps up with her five children..." Mrs. Hansen gouges the pâté with a Ritz cracker. "I'll never know."

Zost comes back with Hansen, and we're all sitting at the redwood deck table, except Hansen. Someone asks Zost about generic drugs. Soon, we're all on the topic of generic drugs. We talk about all aspects of them. Things like which line the doctor needs to sign on to insist on a generic substitute. Chan wonders if you can really save money with generic drugs. He wonders what kind of impurities they have in them. Zost puts his Walkman back on.

I ask Chan to show me his digital watch. I tell him I have a watch just like his. I show him my watch. I say I got my watch at Godfathers' Pizza—just one dollar with the purchase of a large pizza. Chan looks disgusted with me. He says his watch cost him five hundred and fifty bucks at Neiman-Marcus.

Time passes. Nobody's talking much. Hansen's wife is drunk. She jerks her lawn chair close to me, and covers my hand with hers. The Rob Roy in the tumbler in her other hand slops from side to side. She sips hard on her drink; then, she says to me, "Dear," she softens her voice so it's almost gone, "how have you been getting on—I mean so soon after your surgery—if you need anything at all..."

A portion of Mrs. Hansen's Rob Roy spills into her lap. She uses her fingers to flick droplets of it from the tiny hammock formed by her sun dress between her knees. Her knees are white, splayed with blue veins.

Mrs. Hansen goes home. Mr. Hansen is with Zost in the front yard. I see the Chans through the glass slider off the patio sitting on the sofa in Zost's family room. Chan gets up, bends to the TV, and turns through the channels.

Mrs. Zost is making coffee, *the old-fashioned way*, she says, *with a real live percolator*.

I join Zost and Hansen out front. Zost is edging with his gasoline-powered edger. He gives his edges short blasts with the cutter. They sound like volleys from an M-16 rifle. Dirt and grass boil up around his knees. Hansen stands at a respectful distance. I am behind Hansen. Zost pauses. He shuts down the edger and leans on it.

Across the street, I see the García woman come out her front door and walk over to the garage. She's a short, dark-haired woman. She wears a white cotton smock which runs to her ankles. She bends low, nearly to her toes, and hoists the two-cars-wide door, driving into it with her knees until the door lifts and runs upward on its tracks.

Hansen says to me: "This is incredible. That tiny woman is so strong. Does she know she has an automatic Genie opener?"

The García woman starts the Snapper lawn mower. She pushes the Snapper across the driveway to the lawn and arches over it. She budges the mower through the grass, cutting precisely one square section at a time. She steps on the hem of her long white smock, kicks it away, and leans back into the Snapper. The mower juts ahead; the engine burdens and sobs, then whines as it passes over a square of grass.

I cross the street to the García woman. Her back straightens behind the Snapper. She presses a finger against her forehead. She checks her fingertip, and shakes a bead of sweat from it. I look back at Zost and Hansen. Zost leans on his edger. Hansen has his arms folded across his chest.

The García woman smiles. The Snapper idles.

"Let me show you something," I say.

I take her hand from the mower's handle, work the clutch back-and-forth, then walk around the front of the mower. I check to be sure the clutch is out, then I engage the front wheels. I step back behind the Snapper, push the clutch in, cocking the mower at the same time so the front wheels are up. The wheels turn. I disengage the clutch. Then I lower the mower.

Across the street, Zost lights a cigarette.

"See?" I say to her.

"*Sí*," she says, wide-eyed.

She winds a lock of her hair around a finger and places it in her mouth.

I cross the street back to Zost and Hansen. Zost sails his cigarette out to the curb.

"Look what she's doing, man," Zost says.

I turn and look back across the street. The García woman has pushed the clutch in. The Snapper lurches and pulls itself forward. The García woman stands behind it, laughing, looking alternately at me and the Snapper, clapping her hands together. Meanwhile the Snapper wanders, unmanned, on a murderous course across the lawn, over the zinnias, spraying a mixture of purple and yellow bits over the door stoop; the Snapper careens off the tender trunk of an infant palm tree and uproots it; it hugs the sidewalk awhile, then tears out into the street. I start for the AWOL Snapper. Zost tugs at my arm and holds me back.

"Wait a minute, man," he says, "this is terrific."

The García woman stops applauding the Snapper. She's jumping up and down with her fists clenched. She chatters at the Snapper in Spanish. Neighbor kids begin to run in circles around the Snapper, chirping. Then they scatter. A car swerves to avoid the mower. The car jerks to a stop, then peels off, blasting its horn. The Snapper is deflected by the fire hydrant in the Chans' tree lawn, then the metal post of their mail box. It switches directions, climbs the García woman's curb like a miniature M1 Tank, crosses the lawn, bounces into the Crepe Myrtle hedge, and groans against the brick veneer of the house.

Zost shakes his head.

"You can't help that woman, man—you okay?—not too tired? You look tired."

"I'm okay," I say.

The García woman runs over to the Snapper and shuts it off. She leaves the Snapper buried in the hedge.

Zost yanks the starter cord on his edger. The cord whips back into the housing. The tiny engine sputters.

"That's a good one," Hansen says to me.

Zost laughs loudly over the edger.

I go back inside and join Mrs. Zost in her kitchen. She uses an electric knife to slice a London Broil. She uses an exact and even pressure. The beef slivers fall away from the roast easily, in precise portions.

Mrs. Hansen comes in, holding a cup of coffee to her face.

"How are you feeling now, dear?" Mrs. Zost asks her.

Mrs. Hansen smiles behind the cup.

"Much better."

Mrs. Hansen is helping Mrs. Zost with the table settings. Zost is sweeping the grass cuttings from his walk. I stand in the open front door. The sky is oranging now, and the air cooling. The wind has died, and eddies in gentle tides, soft against the skin.

Zost and Hansen are in Zost's garage. I hear Zost's new lathe clunk on, whine as it accelerates, then drone. Soon, there's a screaming sound in the garage as they start cutting wood.

Later, we make short work of the London Broil, cauliflower, and melon slices. Afterward, Mrs. Hansen is helping Mrs. Zost clear the table into the dishwasher, and tanking up again on Rob Roys. The Chans have settled on a television episode of the *Honeymooners*. I don't have to watch it because I already know this episode, the one where Ralph thinks he's going to be the new Manager of the Gotham Bus Company, but in truth, they want him to manage the company softball team.

Ralph is glaring at Alice on the Sony TV when I leave
Zost's house. I hear Ralph say, or I imagine it in part, because
of my familiarity with the episode: "I'll tell you where you're
going to go, Alice—I'll tell you!—you're going to the *moon!
BANG-ZOOM!*"

Later, I'm home. I try to nap on the couch. I roll over a couple
of times on my incision from the operation. I sit up and snap
on the table lamp. There are forty-four tiny marks on my
chest, the scars from the stitches. They have grown purple
and twice their size, like tiny violets. They stand in rank along
a lavender gash.

I go into the bathroom, run cold water through a washcloth, and press the washcloth over the place on my chest
where the incision was made. I go back into the living room,
and sit awhile. I am in my underwear. This seems perfect. I
am too tired to be happy, sad. Then I strip, find a towel, and
wrap it around myself. I'm going to shower. My doctor says it
relaxes me. Good for my circulation.

My doorbell rings. I go to the door and open it.

The García woman stands in the doorjamb. She stares at
my towel.

"Don't help me with the grass anymore," she says.

"You have to guide the mower," I say, "that's all."

The García woman starts to go.

Then she stops.

"It's a joke," she says. "Don't feel bad—it's a joke about
the grass."

Now she looks at my chest.

"They take something out, or put something in?"

"Both."

The García woman smiles and turns to go. Through the
door frame I see her children, standing in the darkened driveway by a big Buick. In the light of the street lamp, their heads

luminesce, changing to black then silver, soft spheres switching color. Her children are patient. Like they're accustomed to waiting for this particular woman.

"Wait," I say to her.

I go to the bedroom and put on my jeans.

I follow the García woman into the night air. A soft light slants out from my front door, over us, and fades at the darkened edges of my lawn.

"So," I say.

"So?"

"So what's new," I say.

"I don't know," the García woman says. "Now I take my babies to the sitter; I go to work...nothing is new, *Señor*."

Zost and his wife come out of their home and stand at their front walk. A light in the front room of the Chans' house suddenly shines. The Hansens' garage door runs up, and the Hansen woman walks out to retrieve a tricycle from their drive. The Hansen woman rolls the tricycle a short distance, then pauses, bent to the tiny handlebars.

New spears of light reach into the street from other homes. I hear a barking dog. The consumptive cough of the García woman's big Buick getting underway. A throb in the pavement. The Zosts talking on their tree lawn. Then Zost himself calls over.

"Hey, man, what's going on?"

I watch the García woman's taillights cast a red glow over the homes one block over.

There is a new moon overhead, a cloudless, burning sky.

El Ojo

I never saw Zoila go off in her wild way, alone, her broad creamy straw hat floating over dark hair to find a *curandero* for me. Perhaps, as the belief goes, she could not find the right person, for only a man named Juan or a woman named Juanita could know the old cures.

And the times she sat atop the *Cleveland and Vicinity* phone book and drove me and my two sisters in our new '63 Fairlane had only been to visit the Sears Lady with red hair heaped on her head like cotton candy. Zoila would scold the Sears Lady for yet another inconvenience, such as the bad timer on the clothes dryer, or the solenoids on the washer, which had gone "wacky," as Zoila put it, and sometimes filled the washer basket with hot water when it should have been cold, and cold when she'd expected hot.

"*Esta máquina idiota no sirve para nada,*" she told the Sears Lady. "I want a whole new machine. I don't want the repairman again. I don't need him to operate on it. Just bring me a whole new machine!"

The Sears Lady at the complaint counter raised an eyebrow, then looked straight at Zoila. And Zoila glared back at her. Then the Sears Lady turned one eye under her high, arched brow to me. Zoila made two-three shuffle steps to my side, placed her hand at the base of my neck and squeezed it.

"Don't—" she said to the Sears Lady. "Don't you look at my baby that way or you'll give him the *ojo.*"

I'm sure the Sears Lady at the complaint counter had no idea what Zoila meant by the *ojo.* Neither did I, but I could not get over how much I disliked Zoila's referring to me as her

"baby." I was every bit of eleven years. But this didn't matter
to Zoila since she had gotten her way, and Father, who I came
to know as curiously unlike Zoila, an automotive engineer at
the Ford Plant in the Golden Days of automotive travel, cared
not to comment on her incessant complaining and her "whole
new machine" outlook. She got results. And results were all
that seemed to matter our first weeks in Cleveland, after moving from Austin, before that Brownsville, and now, with everything new, our surroundings, our machines, I believed she
secretly wished to be back in Brownsville.

The next day a new washer arrived and Zoila was back in
business, washing, ironing, drying diapers, clothes, sheets,
towels—she could clean anything in any quantity, and our
closets were always filled with soft, white, sweet-smelling
things. But even Zoila's sweet-smelling things I knew were
the issue of *las máquinas*, and all of it—the linens, the
mechanical toss and turn of her washer and dryer, the smell
of sweet summer air in my underthings she dried on the line
outside, the great underbellies of jumbo jets as they bore down
on our house and headed for Hopkins Airport, the long sobs of
diesels on the Northwestern tracks a block behind our
house—were all sides of one thing, our new home in the
North, so far from Brownsville, a place that seemed to receive
all things, the smell of burnt diesel, cut grass, people,
machines, nature, no matter how different, thrown together in
one crazy concoction.

Perhaps Zoila never went to find a *curandero* for me
because she was too impatient with anyone or anything that
slowed her household; for each mechanical failure, she had no
desire to know which part broke; the idea of "operating on it,"
as she would often say, seemed to repulse her. She wanted a
whole new machine—no matter what was wrong. And I wanted to know about her revulsion, so I found her sitting at the
table in the kitchen, and asked her, "Why don't you like
repairmen?"

She had spread various counter appliances on the table in front of her. One by one, she took the electric can opener, carving knife, blender, and plugged them into the wall socket. She bent an ear closely to each and listened to the whirring of the motors and mechanisms. When she plugged in the coffee grinder and put it to her ear, I saw her eyebrows lift slightly. She shook the housing and something rattled inside, then she turned the grinder off and looked at it with disgust. I knew it would soon be headed for the grinder graveyard at K-Mart. She nudged the grinder aside, looked at me, and said, "I'll tell you about your little boy uncle."

And she told me a story about my uncle Eduardo, Zoila's younger brother, who, when a boy in Brownsville, had swallowed a poisonous spider. The family was frantic, so they took him to the hospital. All her family were there in the hospital lobby: my grandfather, grandmother, and uncle Eduardo, knowing full well what he had inside him because Zoila had been sure to remind him.

"At the hospital, I put my hands on both sides of Eduardo's head," Zoila explained, and to completely re-enact the scene, she half-stood, reached across the kitchen table, and pressed her palms firmly on both sides of my face. "Like this," she continued, "and I looked him straight in his eyes and said to your little boy uncle, 'You have a poisonous spider inside you—you better hope he does not bite you in your *estómago!*'"

She poked her forefinger into my belly, sat back down on her chair and stared at me as if my life depended on her advice. I was sure she was speaking to me and Eduardo at the same time, talking to both of us over the span of many years.

"Your uncle," she continued, "when I told him this, he knew why we all came to the hospital, but when the lady at the hospital said, 'Who's going to pay?' my father said nothing, and my mother said to him, 'So what can we do?' So my father said, 'We'll take him over to Juan Z.P., the old *curandero*...' and my mother looked hard at my father and said nothing, and Eduardo looked at him and said nothing, so I said, 'All right, let's go! Do you want the spider to bite him in his stomach?'

"So we went to Juan Z.P.'s and told him they wanted so much money for the operation at the hospital, and he said, 'All right, pull his pants down.' So my father pulled Eduardo's pants down. 'Now,' the old *curandero* said, 'bring him out in the yard and lay him down on his stomach.' So we went out into the yard and my father nodded at Eduardo, and he lay down on his stomach. Then Juan Z.P. went inside his house, brought back a bottle of honey, opened it, poured some in his hand, and rubbed it on Eduardo's bare bottom. I was laughing, so my mother made me leave, but I stood inside the doorway of Juan Z.P.'s house and peeped out...then Juan Z.P. picked up a stick from the ground and handed it to my father. 'What do you want me to do?' my father asked Juan Z.P., who replied, 'When the flies gather on his behind, the spider will come out to get them—then you can kill it with the stick.'"

I began to laugh like Zoila had when she saw Eduardo's bare bottom, but this older Zoila looking at me, my mother Zoila, did not laugh. Then she started to smile, but the kind of smile possible only after time puts distance on events. I believe she smiled to let me know her whole story was a gag. Perhaps. But I didn't know, and I tried, as a boy of eleven can only try, to see if it was a gag with my laugh.

"So," I said, "did the spider come out of Eduardo?"

She shifted in her chair, and for the first time since telling me Eduardo's story her eyes wandered back to her stove, her black cast-iron skillet, coffee tins filled with brown, waxy bacon lard she saved for greasing her skillet for tortillas, her twenty-seven potholders hanging from little hooks from the electric exhaust-fan hood, all in different colors, all with little burn spots on them.

More puzzled, I added, "So is this why you don't like repairmen?"

"I got to make supper for your father," she said.

And I knew that if her story had not been a gag, and they had truly taken Eduardo to the crazy *curandero*, then the spider had not come out for the flies on his rump.

Zoila behaved as if the onset of my boyhood illness began with the arrival of Corinne, Father's mother, from Oceanside, California. I expect she felt the usual jealousy a wife feels toward her husband's mother, yet Zoila's scorn for Corinne was more complicated: a troubling distaste for her combined with a puzzling paralysis of spirit. It seemed to come over Zoila all at once. For one thing, Corinne's plane landed at Hopkins Airport in the early afternoon. Father was working, and Hopkins was only a few miles from our house, but I remember her on the telephone with Corinne:

"You can get a taxi—I'm not a very good driver," she said, which startled me because Zoila was anything but shy in an automobile, and in many ways I was grateful that the Fairlane had never stalled iń traffic when Zoila punched the gas pedal, which was her habit, since I was sure she would have next driven directly to the Ford dealership and demanded a whole new Ford!

So Corinne's taxi came a little later in the day; it was raining, another excuse Zoila had used on the phone with Corinne, the slick roads. Corinne emerged from the taxi at the curb in front of our house. She wore a clear plastic rain hat with tiny roses printed on it over her short blonde hair. I did not remember ever meeting my grandmother before this moment, heard only that she was Irish, retired from an administrative job with the Air Force. Her face was marbled with large faint freckles. She had wide blue eyes, long straight teeth, and high, prominent bones in her cheeks. Her fingers were white, fleshy, full of rings of silver and gold, all set with deep red rubies, and I remember seeing the freckles on her knuckles around the handle of her plain brown suitcase with two leather straps.

No one helped her with the suitcase or the rest of her luggage.

When I said, "Hi, Grandma," she didn't respond, and instead moved her tongue all the way around inside her mouth.

She didn't speak to me until we were inside the house. She stripped the rain hat from her head and shook her hair out.

"Well, boy," she said, "let me look at you."

She hugged me and kissed me on my mouth, and I remember her fleshy fingers on my arms, the smell of roses on her neck, and her blue eyes open and looking straight into mine as she kissed me. Since then, I have only opened my eyes once when kissing anyone, avoid kissing in general, but that moment it had been too late, and I was sure that Zoila would again shuffle over to my side and save me, saying, "Don't go kissing him with your eyes open that way or you'll give him the *ojo*."

And I wished she had said this since I believed I was becoming more than a "boy," and I suspected that a grandmother I had seldom met, coming all the way from California, had no business coming so close and kissing me with her eyes open.

When she finished her kiss, I could smell her lipstick—rosy, too—and as she drew back from me, I could see a pale-maroon rouge coating the cells on her skin, near her cheek, where wrinkles ran in vague creases to the corners of her mouth. And at the precise moment Zoila should have warned Corinne not to give me the *ojo*, she instead glanced at Corinne—a dark, quick glance, like a faint glint of light in the blade of a knife—and went into the kitchen. I heard Zoila call out to Corinne a little later, "If you want, you can make some coffee in here."

But Corinne never went into the kitchen to see Zoila, so I stayed with her and the baby Juanita in the living room. Corinne held the baby in her arms. Then Mary, just four-years old, came into the living room and started to point out all the "odd" features of the baby to Corinne: her dark hair, not blonde like Mary's, or, as Mary added, not like Corinne's either. She mentioned the baby's tawny complexion, "really brown," as Mary put it. Next, she commented on the baby's crankiness, thin lips and small mouth that could make such extraordinary noise. Then Zoila came out of her kitchen, took the baby from Corinne, carried her swiftly to her bedroom upstairs, and returned to the kitchen, where I followed her.

I whispered to Zoila: "Shouldn't I take Grandmother's luggage to her room?"

But she did not respond. She remained in her kitchen the rest of the afternoon, and the luggage stayed in the living room with Corinne until Father came home from work.

When I finally followed Father, carrying Corinne's luggage to the extra bedroom upstairs, I wondered about the strange events of that afternoon, things inexplicable to the mind's eye, things that seemed to fall into a hole, a blank aperture without an image when a parent ceases to respond to a child—to me!

Like the name of the place she'd come from, Oceanside, Corinne seemed all too "watery" for my taste—her eyes, her kissing. But I felt badly for her, having come all this way from Oceanside to Cleveland, only to sit with her luggage in our living room. And Zoila's behavior puzzled me: it was one thing to scold a repairman, or the mail carrier, or the gas-meter reader, the host of callers who kept our house in the good graces of the city, but another to greet my father's mother so poorly. Besides, in some ways I was strangely attracted to the woman of roses from the land of sun. She seemed to be made of light,

and fine, textured, freckled skin—and freckled stories: she
told me she had seen UFO's, like brown spots below the
clouds, flying among the hills east of Oceanside and west over
the Pacific.

So while Zoila was cooking or off to J.C. Penney's returning pants or baby clothes that did not fit, or whose buttons
had come loose, I'd knock softly at Corinne's door. She never
answered, not once, but I could hear her moving in the room,
and when I slowly pushed her door inward, she'd be there on
her bed, her suitcase on the nightstand beside her, always
open. Though she didn't speak to me when I first came in, I
would in time work my way over to the suitcase, asking her
kid stuff all the while, stuff Father, the engineer, had mentioned to me about time and space, relativity, the way one
might be able to stop aging, or actually grow younger by traveling at or in excess of the speed of light. I knew all the questions to ask, just to get a peek inside her ever-open suitcase.
But after a couple of tries I got nowhere. She would reach over
and unceremoniously close the lid. On my third unsuccessful
try, she got up, went to her dresser, opened the top drawer,
and removed a copy of *Life* magazine. She went back to her
bed and sat with the magazine on her lap. Then she patted
the bed with one palm for me to come sit beside her. I did,
eventually, after carefully weighing my curiosity about the
magazine against the possibility that she'd kiss me again on
my lips with her eyes open. But my curiosity won.

So I sat near her on the bed while she fingered the edges
of limp, glossy pages, turning them slowly until she found a
page with two photographs, one showing the tops of trees and
a cigar-shaped object nosing down into them. The other photograph, very grainy, showed several small discs over water.
She ran one hand over the page and spoke in a far-off voice.

"Here, you see, it's all possible," she said. "These space-
ships can take you to other worlds, beyond, places where there
are people like you and me, but people who have accumulated

the knowledge of many centuries, great scientists, like your father.... You see," she added, "they are enlightened."

The photographs of UFO's were all very interesting, but I still wanted to get near that suitcase, so later that week, on my fourth try, I got a good look inside when Corinne turned away from me a moment, took a bullet-shaped lipstick from her purse and screwed the stick up. But what I saw in the suitcase was a great disappointment: a few underthings, no big deal since I'd seen plenty of Zoila's hanging on the line in full sun, and a couple books whose titles meant little to me, one, *The Perfect and True Perfection of the Philosopher's Stone by the Brotherhood of the Gold and Rosy Cross*, and the other, *Rosicrucian Principles for Home and Business*. But all this was far less important than what I discovered when I looked back at Corinne. She looked at me, smiling with her maroonish cheeks and her new, red lips. She knew I'd been into her suitcase with my eyes, and I expected her to then do what grown-ups always did, to reach into the suitcase, and say, "Do you want to see what's in there? Here, I'll show you. Now, this is..." But she didn't. She rolled slightly to one side of the bed, tapped her ruby nails on the open lid of the suitcase, then shut it, all the while staring and smiling at me. Then she tucked her arms under her breasts and said, "You are one of the Hidden Masters of the Rosy Cross."

Like the Sears Lady with the piled red hair, Corinne lifted her right eyebrow and looked at me a long time with a startling gaze full of stern wonder. Then Zoila appeared at Corinne's door.

"What are you doing looking at him that way?" Zoila said.

"Nothing," Corinne said. "I don't know what you mean."

"You know what I mean.... You...you.... Don't go looking at my baby that way!"

Zoila shuffled to my side, stuck her fingers on my neck, and pulled me around the foot of the bed to the door. Corinne sat placidly with her hands in her lap and looked out her window, and I was hustled into my room at the other end of the upstairs hallway. Zoila put her hands firmly on my shoulders and pushed me down until I sat on the edge of my bed. Then she pressed a hand to my forehead.

"You're sick," she whispered. "You're burning up."

"I'm not," I complained, partly because I didn't feel sick, and partly because I knew she'd soon be feeding me curatives, such as onion sandwiches and fried garlic. She'd be forcing cup after cup of aniseed tea into me. She'd done it before, once, when I had the measles, luckily only three-day measles, not the kind lasting a fortnight. "I'm not sick, Mama," I persisted, using the familiar term for 'Mother' with her, hoping she'd be touched and show me a little mercy. But she replied: "You're sick.... You stay here and don't get up. I'll make you a nice onion sandwich and some tea."

So there I was, as Corinne had called me, one of the Hidden Masters, in a state of confounded humiliation, wishing oddly that for once Father, that invisible engineer, would show up and purge our house of the intermingling scents of Corinne's roses and Zoila's onions.

And Zoila's cure began, her regimen for my illness, whatever it was. Onions, so pungent and watery in my mouth that when I thought about them tears formed in my eyes—even before their white, ominous rings appeared between slices of bread. And aniseed tea, mild to the taste, but running straight through me and, with the taste of onion already in my mouth, becoming like a bitter licorice, hot and numbing to my lips. After a couple days, I guessed that my sickness was caused by the *ojo* Corinne had given me. But so awful was my cure for Corinne's *ojo*, I thought more than once about sneaking back into Corinne's room to ask her if I could get a ride on one of her *Life* flying saucers. Any place would do. A one-way ticket...

While I was in my bedridden state, I enlisted Mary to collect news about Zoila. Several times I was sure I heard Mary
pacing about outside my door, spying on me.

"Come in here, Mary," I said. "Come here, all right?"

Mary came in and nudged the door closed with her
behind.

"Tell me…what's Mama doing?"

"You're sick," she said.

"No, I'm not."

"Mama says you're burning up."

"Just come over here—and shut up."

She came over to my bed and stood with a worried look on
her face.

"Where's Mama?" I asked.

"She put the lawn mower in the car and took it back to
the Sears Lady."

"All right…go away," I said, and she left, putting one tiny
finger on the doorknob and quietly pulling the door closed.

I waited a few minutes, then left my room and walked to
Corinne's door. I knocked softly with one knuckle and listened. If I stood outside her door long enough, I had always
been able to detect the rustle of her clothes or the working of a
spring in the bed, but now there was no sound in her room,
and suddenly I felt as though the world might have changed,
or somehow shifted, a bit like the way an earthquake seems to
displace the air all at once, causes a little explosion, all the air
suddenly rushing inches to a new place. Was it possible that
Corinne had gone with Zoila to Sears to return the lawn
mower? It seemed to me that this would have been a wonderful sort of reconciliation, and I saw a bright future for us
all.… Corinne would bring her mysterious old book about perfection and philosophers' stones, her photographs of UFO's,
and spread them out in the living room. Zoila would join her
with her herbs, onions, garlic, aniseed, her queer little cures
she had gathered from her mother, and she would tell *las ta-
llas*, tales she'd heard as a girl, some about the *curanderos*,

jokes people would say to one another sitting in a circle on her porch around an old cooler with ice packed around tall bottles of Superior beer...and I again wondered if Zoila's story about my little boy uncle and the spider had been a joke.

I pushed Corinne's door open. She wasn't inside. But in just two days her room was transformed. She had borrowed books from the library—piles of all heights covered her bed, dresser, the nightstand near her suitcase, the floor in corners of the room, books such as Korzybski's *Science and Sanity*. And she had filled the room with lamps, long-necked desk lamps, globe lamps, hurricane lamps—all burning above the stacks of books. It was an odd scene, especially in full summer light. I moved to one corner of her room, near the window, and out it saw Corinne below, lying on the yellow-webbed chaise lounge in the back yard. She was sunning herself, wearing a two-piece swimsuit, white, printed with tiny pink roses. She had drawn a towel over her face. Despite her freckles I was surprised to see how white and firm her body looked. She was a young grandmother, for Father himself was young. Zoila was younger than Corinne or Father, though I often found it hard to believe Zoila could be described by something as simple as age.

Corinne had oiled herself, and the sun high above made little pins of light glance off her thighs, and I saw the same strange light reflected from the rings on her fingers and from her toes painted dark red, so red they seemed black, making them appear metallic.

Corinne shifted slightly in the chaise. She reached under the towel covering her face, lifted one end of it, and made a little tent. I started to back away from the window, but soon realized her little tent made a safe bit of shade over her eyes, so I was in no danger of her seeing me. But suddenly she drew back the little tent and, revealing one eye, stared up at me. All of it, the pins of light glinting off her toes and rings and white oiled skin, the roses and her single eye that suddenly gave its light to me, paralyzed me.... I dashed from the window and her room.

I took to my bed feeling my forehead with my palms, thinking I might be a little feverish, slept the rest of the afternoon with what I was sure was fever, and woke only when I heard Zoila in her Fairlane with the lawn mower poking out the open trunk come onto the driveway.

Evening, I could smell Zoila's enchiladas cooking, sat up in bed, and waited, hoping she'd bring me the substance of the corny, meaty smell, but she came into my room with a TV tray loaded with an onion sandwich, a cup of aniseed tea, a small plate of fried garlic, a wedge of lemon, and a tiny glass filled with water. I drooped, slumped back into my bed, and she set the tray on my knees. She put the wedge of lemon in my mouth. Then she placed one hand on top of my head, the other under my chin, and pressed my jaws together until the acidic juice trickled into my mouth. When I could stand the bitter taste no longer, I spit the wedge onto the bed.

"Why do I have to eat all these things?" I said.

But the woman was unshakable. She calmly picked the spent wedge out of my bed sheets and placed it on the tray.

"I'll tell you about an old man who was a *curandero*," she said, sat on the bed near me, and handed me the onion sandwich. "They brought him a man who had a sickness in his stomach. And the old *curandero* said, 'Give him goat turds.'"

"Goat turds?" I asked.

"Yes," Zoila said, nudging a few cloves of fried garlic at me. "Boiled goat turds.... Well, they gave him the goat turds and he got well with them. Then one of the man's friends said to the old *curandero*, 'We never could find out what was wrong with him, so how'd you know to give him goat turds?' 'Well,' the old *curandero* replied, 'Since goats eat all kinds of weeds and herbs, I knew the cure would be there in the turds.'" Zoila reached for the fried garlic, took a bit in her fingers, set it on my tongue, and pinched my lips together. "Now, *mi bebé*, you eat all this stuff."

She put her hand to my forehead, ran it across my head and back of my neck, and with one last characteristic pinch of my cheek, rose from the bed and left.

The next morning, I heard Father showering, water running in the pipes, then his footfalls on the floorboards outside my door. I wanted to peek out to see him, wanted him to come in, but he did not, and a little later I wondered what he could have possibly said to make everything better, because I had started to believe, as Zoila did, that I had become feverish, and the wildest possible assortment of potential cures would be necessary to find the one that would work—but where—or what—was this cure?

After a short while, I heard voices at the other end of the hallway, then Father's footsteps go off in that direction, but not his voice; then the voices were silent, and I heard him go out the front door and leave in his Corvair. I waited a long time, perhaps an hour or so while my curiosity rose, then I opened my door, saw that the upper hall was clear and walked to Corinne's door.

I tapped softly on Corinne's door with one knuckle and listened. When I was sure there would be no reply, I went inside. Corinne stood by the same window from which I had spied her the day before. She was dressed in the same things she wore the day she arrived, complete with her plastic rain hat printed with roses, her rose perfume. Her rose-colored sunglasses covered her blue eyes, and her suitcase on the nightstand was closed, her things packed. The room was filled with books, as before, but her lamps were not burning. She turned a little to me, bent slightly at her knees, reached down to the floor, and took the electrical cord of one lamp in her hand. She held it out to me.

"Look what your crazy mother has done," she demanded.

I looked all around the room at the floor and saw that all the electrical cords to the lamps had been neatly sliced in two. When I turned my attention back to Corinne, she leaned over a little and kissed me on my mouth, the lenses of her rosy glasses coming in close. I held my eyes open once more—but could not find her eyes, just the opaque, shadowy panes of red in my field of vision. She then took her suitcase by the handle and left.

"Remember," she said, "you are one of the Hidden Masters."

After I heard Corinne go out the front door and her taxi drive away, I stood in her room a long while, gradually sensing that the vague smell of roses gave itself over to the sweet air of summer mornings. The place where I lived, the place I had been so sure received all things was suddenly silent, and in that pause, no jets cut the sky, no diesels drummed the air...

That evening I fell asleep without the fits of two nights before, without the heat I imagined in my head. The room was hot, the air stiff and wet, but in the thick air I seemed cool and loose, and I slept on my back, musing once before I dropped off that I would sleep like a dead boy...

I woke very late in the night, and in weak light through my eye slits I saw Zoila leaning over me. In one hand she held an unbroken raw egg, and when I closed my eyes briefly she passed the smooth, cool skin of the egg over my face. After a time of passing the egg over my forehead and cheeks, she whispered, "Open your eyes and look at me."

I kept my eyes shut tightly, feigning sleep, wondering whether Zoila had a tray with her, and on it a late night snack of onion sandwiches.

But once again my curiosity overpowered me, so I looked at her.

She held the egg carefully with two fingers, inches from my face.

"You see?" she said. "I have made the *ojo* come out of you and go into this egg.... Now, look at me and tell me what you see."

So I looked at her, her brown eyes set in her small oval and olivaceous face, framed in short dark hair and the blackness and thickness of the air; I wanted to say, "Mama, I don't see anything." That would have been the truth—but instead I said to her, "Don't look at your baby or you'll give him the *ojo*."

"Look," she insisted.

So I had to tell her...

"I don't see anything," I said, and growing irritated, added, "just my crazy mama."

"I know," she said. "So I will tell you what you don't see. You don't see Eduardo's bare, honied rump in the heat of Brownsville; or my tongue, my Spanish tongue and my mother's tongue; or bare feet and dark backs pushing against the heavy air; you don't see sights and sounds that are hidden from you.... But you see me—me, yes? And you don't see no rosy crosses and no *máquinas idiotas*, right?"

Zoila took her tray of curatives away, and later that night I tried to sleep, but what I believe was the beginning of a new fever caused me to toss and turn in bed until I could bear it no longer. And when I woke I cried because I could not sleep, because all the things around me were so terribly familiar, a jet groaning overhead, the scent of diesel in the summer air out my window, buttons clacking against the steel hull of the clothes dryer. I cried because my sheets smelled so fresh and felt cool and dry. I cried because I could not see the terribly unfamiliar things Zoila told me were there in her eyes, not knowing why, only knowing I was burning up because Mama had given me her *ojo*, me, the Hidden Master of things quite hidden from me. I was burning because the baby Juanita was crying in her crib in another room, and because she would not come, nor would anyone ever come to fix things the way I wanted them, because Mama had given me her *ojo*, and because I have carried the sweet affliction all my life.

Corpus

Inhabitants of the city call *Corpus Christi* simply *Corpus*, body itself. They tear *Christi* from the body, disconnect it so only the body remains, but not because the words make the tongue tired. Had not *Corpus-Christi* been torn apart, the tongue would have made the same /K/, same voiceless velar stop, twice, in that part of the velum that feels more articulate, the place where the bone becomes soft and the sound hard....

I was born in Corpus, separated from it thirty years and all the blind, infinite avenues in between...and now *Corpus sans Christi* seems only a cadaver comprised of hard consonants and droning, open vowels...yet the sound of the body itself, dead and inanimate, still drags things from me: my Mexican mother, who made the mightiest tortillas in the Western World, who as I slept anointed my forehead with olive oil and ran cold eggs over my face to draw out evil spirits when I was sick, who I believe became insane when she never returned to Corpus; my father who fled the gigantic Lone Star State with cold, colossal dreams of space exploration in the research labs and crowded cities of the north; my brothers and sisters, who, like the native Karankawa Indians, the Water Walkers of Corpus, now seem to live their lives looking for new places to pass among the waves, shallow reefs and transitory strips of shifting sand that pile up and vanish with the tides along the coasts and inseams of archipelago islands. They spend their lives looking for invisible, elusive bridges to walk upon, to confound their enemies, to bring something bright and new to their tired families...Corpus...how cruel that I let the years pass; how cruel that all my blood have fled, or died, or lost their way; how cruel they let the years pass, and passed from the body; how alone, how suddenly alone...

Yet I return to Corpus, though I wonder which of so many paths has led me here, permitted my return. Is it the idea that hurricanes of 1874, 75, 86, and of 1900, 16, 19, 33, 41, and the names of their angry twisting souls, *Allen, Beulah, Carla, Celia,* have blown away the old faces of *El Rincón*—the Bend, the Corner, the Front of Sand that shows itself to the Gulf? Is it the idea that the crippled and kidnapped landscape—scoured so many times—will now accept me? Has the land forgotten my absence as it has forgotten the faces of the sand, storm after storm? Has my sin of absence been washed away?

Or am I really here in Corpus? Am I really east of the city with my feet, my legs in Corpus Christi Bay? I have my senses. I have the elements around me. A fine sun in the west warms my back to the center of my body. A stiff wind blows inland from the bay. The blue water of the bay is in my eyes, in my mind. The sand is in my feet. The elements are around me, in me. But who will say these elements are *Corpus*? Can these elements swirl and toss and mingle so intimately they make a place particular: sun heating water, water driving wind, wind and water shaping earth? Can these elements work this way in my body, in my Corpus, *are* my Corpus, or are, for a stretch of time upon my return, *the* Body?

But how can these elements be the Body? Our family is not part of the Body: my father, buried with a modest, flat VA stone on a knoll in Greensburg, PA; my sister, married to a rubber engineer in Akron; my brother in Wyoming drinking off a dishonorable discharge; my tiny dark-haired mother in Salt Lake City, halfway in a place for the disturbed, halfway out, coming, going, going, coming; she revolves; it all revolves, as if the blood lines in all their locations over the planet circumscribe the earth as it turns with red ink, in different lines of latitude, drawing parallel orbits, lines of circular and infinite length, eternally returning to Greensburg and Akron and

Bozeman and Salt Lake.... The laws of physics work against
us...parallel lines never, never, never...

One line...Father was a physicist for NASA. The year
after Neil Armstrong landed on the Moon, Father landed in
the intensive care unit. Four more years and he was gone.
Then came Velcro and other benefits no one ever imagined the
Space Program could have produced...side benefits.... Space
was Father's final frontier, and now, now as I stand on the hot
and blinding back of Corpus, is it mine? Why not just leave,
cruise by like Alonso de Piñeda, who reportedly sighted the
bay and simply named it *Corpus Christi*, then sailed off. Oh,
the ease of it...

I wade into the ocean, wary of Portuguese men-of-war and
their black whip stingers. No one in the wide blue bay is with
me. I see the jetty. The breakwater turns like a snake south
into the bay, away from the sea wall with its Mayan steps
that lead directly to the water. The snake runs east, stretches
for the Gulf, the uncertain line of Mustang Island, and the
more uncertain breach, the tip and terminus of the archipelago island, nearly indistinguishable in the humid distance:
Aransas Pass. I turn and turn in the tepid water. I believe I
have lost my legs. The water slaps my chest, again, again....
The breeze never fails; it pushes, pushes waves onto shore. A
small fish skips over the crest of a wave, and I see others
inside the crests of waves. Their noses bend into the thicker
part of one crest, riding, riding, until the wave crashes into
my chest...how alone, how easy to forget the thousands of
others in the Body on shore. How terribly empty, how beautiful the new and empty world must have seemed to Piñeda.
Who could blame him for uttering such a name, *Corpus
Christi*?... How could the man, with the weight of Europe
slouching on him, the centuries of dogma leaning at his back,
trapped, and riding the wave of discovery, rolling forward
from the east, how could such a man reach back into his soul
and pull anything out but *Corpus Christi*? The bay and beach-
es must have made quite an impression—and me?—what

should I call it? How do I stand here, with no excuse, no others leaning or slouching at my back.

My body betrays me: my tongue, wind, water, fire, earth, the eyes of ancient explorers all betray me, so I approach Corpus from the west, inland.... All around me are brown and wrinkled people. I follow Old Brownsville Road, broken asphalt, limp and desiccated grasses impossibly pushing up from the conglomerate of stone and asphalt softened by the glare of the sun. Where are the seeds of the grasses? Where are they? *Embriones desecados*, will you tell me *your* story?

I find a set of old railroad tracks, creosoted ties, bent and worn and buried in broken shells and misshapen fossils. What were these? In which warm, shallow sea did they live?

I follow the tracks away from the road. I walk among the real people. They chatter in Spanish around me. They eat *lenguas y tripas y carne guisada*. The land is hot and over-paved and suffers. Still, the palms and yucca and prickly pears persist among interstices of broken pavement. What more will show through? What can I possibly recognize—my *Corpus*?

The dogs drag the garbage into the street behind Villarreal's Lounge. A rusted quarter panel hangs off a pickup parked at the Majestic Club. The truck is old, funereal. The Majestic is old. Bars brace the windows of shanties. A fan props open the front door of one shanty, turning, turning hot air into hot air. There are children at La Estrella, a bakery. They hold their arms out for sweet bread, and they are shooed away. I see into the houses on Espinozo, Sabina, Verbeena streets, where women carry and bounce their children against their chests. On a corner a man sleeps with his head half-tucked in the wheel well of his truck. The melons in his truck are dirt cheap. The melons are good and my money is not. There are couches and easy chairs under the eaves of the

shanties. Stuffing rises from their cushions in fantastic
plumes. A chrome bar stool, pocked with rust, glitters in the
sun, glitters, glitters...and here is the impossible way of my
race, the beauty of my abandoned tongue, *mi lengua materna*,
the tongue boiled and eaten, *las lenguas*, the tongue eaten and
swallowed; here is the tongue digested and made shit; here is
the music of tongues made shit; how can I name my people,
my people who eat the insides of beasts?

I can hardly know a logic, even a way of doubtful accep-
tance. But can I accept this Corpus even if I find it? Can I ever
take the dust and stench, alien music, dogs who display the
cost of everything in the streets?

An army of fire ants run over my feet, and I can no longer
stand at the place where my grandparents' house must have
stood. He was the most skilled of billboard painters; she the
maker of mighty tortillas...the cost of everything, the essence
of cost, the name of the cost, the cost of names. How can I
name this? *Corpus*? Rotting and desperate and voiceless Corpus? Silent and impossible *Christi*?

I step up to the tiny door of the shanty of S. Vásquez. A
barefoot man in jeans and a t-shirt stands behind the floor fan
in the door.

"*Perdóneme*," I say. "*Busco una casa...la casa de Durant.*"

S. Vásquez stares at me. The light is at my back. I am not
sure he sees me. My face must be hidden. My face must seem
unforgivably dark. He places his hands on the top of the fan
and leans forward.

"*¿Quién es?*"

"*La casa de Durant...¿dónde está?*"

"*Váyase*," he whispers, and disappears into the shanty.

Farther inland. Sunday mass, a mission church, Church of the
Holy Family. Vague fractures fan over its frontispiece, from
the corner of the door and window boxes—all over-paved with

thin, pinkish plaster: something new. Outside, an old tradition, the Stations of the Cross, Way of the Cross, the road
Jesus followed.... *Via Dolorosa...La Strada...Sorrowful
Way...Cruysgang...Via Crucis...* I prefer *La Strada.* I am
thinking of an indulgence, something to exchange for the fat
plenary of all my sins—what are they? The sins of absence?
The absent son? Are not all things forgotten? Even sins?

I feel a scapular in my pocket made of plain white felt
folded over a gold braided cord, run my fingers over the vague
relief of the image of Christ. I carry my little sacramental all
these thirty years, from sock drawer to glove box, from brief-
case to bank security box, even among the silverware. I feel
the rough faded print, faded Jesus, halo, there, in my pocket,
yoke of Christ...and I took it off, can't remember taking it off,
knew not what it meant to remove it from my shoulders. I was
young. I let the years pass. I see the world of woe and mistake,
of neglect and shivering night, the souls living in the shadows.
Sunday silence. Lamb slaughtered and plastic-wrapped with
packets of mint jelly for the common consumer.... How can
the slaughtered Lamb take away the sins of the world?

Inside the Church of the Holy Family I smell incense,
prayers already ascended to heaven with the airy residues of
smoldering resins. Am I too late? Do I have intentions? I have
none...only, I am here. Sunday. Corpus, after thirty years'
absence.... The priest holds his vestments high. They drape
his arms and trail along the wooden floor. He gently pinches
the Host, Body of Christ, between his fingers, then sets the
Body aside and raises the cup filled with the Host above its
corporal. He will speak, break the silence, offer me the Body...

I kneel in front of the priest and hear him name the place,
here is Corpus Christi, and I eat my sins of absence, *here is the
Body of Christ*, and I take the road, the dolorous way, and
each of the passions along it into my mouth. I eat my tongue,
swallow my people, swallow the garbage of my people after
the dogs have dragged it into the streets and licked it clean. I
eat fire burning water, water driving wind, wind shaping

earth. I eat until the plenum of my woe and mistake is full and fat, until there, on my knees before the priest, in a single square of light from a window over the altar, I present my tongue, and upon it all I have eaten is dancing and ready—and then he places the Body on my tongue with every-thing else there, and I draw it inside and raise it to the spot at the roof of my mouth—the soft place of hard sounds, place where, if not for the hard and vanishing Body between my tongue and velum I might then make the initial voiceless stop, and the word, *Corpus,* and the second coming word, *Christi,* and the open and closed vowels that complete and name the thing that silences all—and there allow it to melt, to vanish and dissolve in the darkness behind and below my eyes...

Then I make proper sorrow. I wonder, *Is such a vanishing Body good? Do you prefer its taste?* I touch the priest's vest-ments, reach out with my hand, and say, *I am trying to come home. May I have another? One more? And another?*—until his trembling cup is finished.